DRAGON RUNNERS BK 2

STUD

ML NYSTROM

STUD © 2018 by ML NYSTROM

For information, contact the publisher, Hot Tree Publishing.
www.hottreepublishing.com

Editing by Hot Tree Editing
Cover design by Claire Smith
Book design by Inkstain Design Studio

ISBN: 978-1-925655-83-4
10 9 8 7 6 5 4 3 2 1

MORE FROM ML NYSTROM

Mute

Stud

Blue

To every woman who has been judged by appearance,
attitude, occupation, age, or life choices, you are all beautiful!
Don't let the world pigeonhole you. Dare to dream!

CHAPTER ONE

"**F**uck my life!" **Almost ten** o'clock. I was sitting at the bar alone waiting for my older brothers Patrick and Angus to show up. They were twins and only a year older than me, but acted like they were still in high school, partying and playing as much as possible. After finishing up work at the job site today, both pushed me into meeting them here to drink a little, hang out, and check out the live music. The Dragon Runners Motorcycle Club had rented this empty storefront in Bryson City to serve as a temporary River's Edge bar until the new and improved one could be finished. I had been looking forward to a night alone in my tiny house, but of course I showed up on time at the bar, and of course I was still waiting for them forty minutes later. I glanced at my watch again. Make that forty-five minutes. Useless *fecks* the both of them!

I sipped on the whisky shot I'd bought along with the pint of Guinness. It burned with a smooth, smoky fire down the back of my throat. Da always said it was a waste of good whisky to shoot it all back at once.

"Sip it with respect, lads!" he would say before he tapped the glass on the bar top and took his first taste of the night. My father was full-blooded Irish, born in America to parents of the old country who came over to Ellis Island decades ago. He'd been taught Gaelic as a kid and even though he'd never set foot in Ireland, he still insisted on talking with a slight brogue, touted all things Irish, including naming all his children with Irish names. I had five brothers. Conner was the oldest and the one I was closest to. Next were Owen and Garrett the first set of twins. Angus and Patrick were the second set and the bane of my existence with their pranks and tricks. My name is Eva and I got the dubious pleasure of being the youngest and only girl. Fergus MacAteer was our father.

Da rarely came to the bars anymore, usually only after the job was finished. He'd buy a round for us saying a job well done and smoke one of his smelly cigars. Connor came out once in a while, but that too was rare. Garrett and Owen headed out to a different bar, as they only wanted to drink and didn't want music to disturb that activity. Therefore, I was left with Patrick and Angus, neither of them with me at the moment. They probably stopped after work and spent more time than I did getting spiffed up, hoping to impress someone enough to get laid tonight. I briefly wondered how pathetic I looked, sitting at the bar alone, still dressed in what amounted to work clothes, drinking by myself. It didn't particularly bother me that I was alone, but my preference would have been to stay in and enjoy my own company. After spending all day at a job site with my brothers, I'd usually had all the loving family time I could stand without punching someone. However, I did like live music. I'd showered off the grime and sweat from the day, but just thrown on what I planned to wear tomorrow. I hadn't had a chance to go to the laundromat, and I didn't have a lot of choices at the moment—or at least ones that would fit with a biker bar. Jeans, a plain dark blue tank top, and a light green chambray work shirt with our company name "Pub Builders" across the back just above a dark green shamrock. I occasionally called it a clover just to watch Da get spitting mad.

My father, brothers, and I were a family business of pub and bar builders. It was what we were known for and what we traveled most of the East Coast doing. Sometimes we got hired to remodel and sometimes for a complete rebuild, like the one we were doing now for this motorcycle club. I'd heard from some of the locals the place blew up in some sort of biker war. I didn't know a lot of details, only hoped the war was over and no one would be trying to blow up the new bar. Especially while we were at the job site building it! *I don't do drama.*

I finished sipping the shot and lightly pushed the glass toward the bar edge. I could see from the corner of my eye the band setting up for the night. The lead singer and bass player, Stud, caught my attention and I quickly looked away. I met him the first day we were on the job site. There was no other way to describe him other than Viking god. Tall, broad shoulders, long blond hair with just enough wave, ice-blue eyes, and just plain hot. Even better, he was *smart!* College degrees in accounting and law. I was lucky just to have a high school diploma. The bar's owner, Betsey, and her business partner, Mute, were the ones who hired us to rebuild it. Stud was the one who was taking care of getting us paid. I'd seen a few of the other club members and heard a few other names but hadn't met them yet to put faces with them. I knew Stud was a road name and he had a different one on his driver's license, but I didn't know what it was. From what I'd seen so far, Stud definitely fit him.

We'd been here for about a week. The cleanup of what was left of the old building was complete and the new foundation laid. Stud and Betsey had met us at the site on the day we arrived. Betsey quickly became one of my favorite people with her dyed red hair, high-heeled boots, her loud Southern accent, and her no-nonsense attitude. She was super friendly, super nice, had a super strong personality, and was the club's matriarch. I had thought on more than one occasion that I wanted to be her when I grew up. Stud had shown up on his tricked-out Harley. I'd felt its rumble in my gut and immediately had the urge to jump on the machine to see how much power it had.

"Nice to meet you, Eva," he had said in a low, seductive voice while looking directly into my eyes. He'd clasped my hand and shook it firmly. His beautiful face had a half smile on it that was meant to be part real and part flirty. I merely nodded and smiled back. "Player," my inner voice said in a bitchy tone. I'd been around a lot of beautiful men in my travels with my family and had grown immune to them. I could appreciate beautiful men, but there was always a big scene when they were around. *Did I mention I don't do drama?*

Stud had come by several times this past week and would always greet us. He would set up his computer and papers in the work trailer, and spent the day working on whatever stuff he worked on. Why he didn't do this at the club's compound, the Lair, I didn't know. Women came by to see him constantly, some bringing him food or coffee. He did his smiley thing and flirted a lot, and I watched how he touched and treated them. He really was a player, but when he was with a woman, she had all his attention. I never saw him talk down to one, or treat them with anything less than respect, but it was clear (at least to me) that he was not going to settle on just one. My brothers certainly didn't mind the constant flow of females at the job site, and frankly, they could take lessons from Stud. Did I mention the twins had taken the art of "player" to a new level?

The screech of feedback had me looking up at the tiny raised stage. Stud was frowning. He turned and bent over to make an adjustment to the sound equipment. I got an eyeful of his finely sculpted ass—until the skank blocked me. I had seen her come by the job site often, and decided she was *not* one of the beautiful people. Her hair was huge and blonde, but it looked like the fried blonde you got from a bottle and huge because it was teased up and lacquered into place. It didn't move around a lot. Her clothes were biker-slut chic. Short jean skirt, black cowboy boots, tiny white tank top two sizes too small with a Harley logo on the front, and a black push-up bra showing through the thin material.

I watched as she placed her hand right on his fine ass and copped a feel. He turned with a frown and said something to her. She responded back, leaning into the stage, her arms close together and I imagine her cleavage was pushed up. Apparently she'd been doing some serious drinking already as she was wobbling a bit on her stacked heels. Stud shook his head and said something else. She responded again, tilting her head and almost falling over. This went on for a few minutes until I saw him close his eyes, relax his face, and chuckle as if saying "I give up," and nod. She jumped and clapped, and I heard her let out a squeal of triumph. I took another sip of beer to keep from rolling my eyes. There's no way I'd ever squeal for anything.

I looked at my watch again and growled. I'd been sitting there waiting for my brothers for over an hour. *Fuck this!* I downed the last of my beer. I was about to leave when the bar noise got deafeningly louder. The band started playing an old Garth Brooks song about friends in low places. Stud was the front man, singing into a mic, thumping his bass, and winking at the crowd. He was really putting on a show, drawing everyone's attention and had a bevy of young women dancing, whooping, and shaking in front of him, including the bleached blonde—surprise!

The band was good, and it had been a long time since I got to hear live music. I raised my hand to the bartender for another beer, deciding to stick around for a little longer.

Stud had the crowd eating out of his hand as the band moved from song to song. I watched him work the instrument, stroking the neck lovingly, smiling at the women around him with those Nordic blue eyes. He wore jeans, like 90 percent of the crowd, but topped it with a burgundy Henley that showed off his broad shoulders and gave a hint of how defined his chest and abs were. He wore his leather club cut over that but I expected he'd lose it eventually. Those stage lights were hot and he was probably sweating. He wasn't muscle-bound huge, but he was definitely built, as my brothers would say, like a brick house.

The band segued into another country tune by Rascal Flatts this time. I sipped at my fresh beer and stared. He really was magnificent. I was far enough into my own head that he caught me watching him. His blue eyes met mine and he gave me that half smile like he knew I'd been admiring him and shared a special secret with only me. He jerked his chin and winked at me. I nearly choked and ended up swallowing more than I wanted.

I gave him a nod back, trying to play it cool. He turned his attention to the bouncing woman in front of him, one with black hair on the top of her head and bright blue from her ears down. I pondered for a bit if that was by design or if she was growing it out.

The band was really good, not just because of the appeal of the Viking front man. The guitarist ran riffs like nobody's business and the drummer was tight in sync with Stud on the bass. All of them had nice voices and when they harmonized together, I bet more than one set of panties melted. Before I knew it, another forty-five minutes had passed and my fucking brothers still hadn't shown up.

"We're going to take a short break," Stud said into the mic, smiling at the crowd and winking. Damn, he really knew how to work it! Even slightly sweaty from the heat on the stage, he was beautiful. He exited the stage through the back, disappearing to the screams and whoops of the bouncing biker bunnies at the front.

I glanced at my watch again.

Fuck my life, I'm done with this! I got up from the barstool, taking quick inventory of my condition. Three beers and two whisky shots wasn't much in a hard-drinking Irish family, and I felt okay to drive my truck back to the job site where my tiny house was parked. Still, it was a lot and I needed to break the seal, so I went to find the restrooms.

I made my way through a side room, passing by some other bikers in Dragon Runners cuts shooting pool and playing darts, to a narrow hallway where the restrooms were located. A big bald member was lining up a difficult shot and I waited until he stroked his cue stick before moving around him. The nine ball sank in the side pocket with a click, and he raised his fist over his head with a crow of victory.

"Whoo! Take that, you fucker! Ha! Oops!" He finally noticed me. "'Scuse me, baby."

He wore a tank under his club cut showing off his bulky arms and brightly colored tattooed sleeves. His head was shaved but his mouth was framed in a dark brown Fu Manchu with a chin duster. Not drop-dead gorgeous like Stud, but still good-looking.

"No problem, big guy. Nice shot by the way," I commented, hoping he wouldn't want to strike up a conversation. I just wanted to pee and get home.

"Thanks, baby." His brown eyes roamed my plainly clad body from my head to my tooled leather toes. "You want to shoot a game later? I'll be glad to teach you."

I smiled and raised my eyebrows devilishly. Maybe I'd take him up on the offer sometime just to see his face when I cleared the table. In building bars for a living, well, let's just say I knew a thing or two about pool.

"Maybe another night. I'm hitting the head and getting home.

Gotta work tomorrow on getting your real bar finished so you can move back in," I said, squeezing between him and the wall.

"*You're* on the construction crew?" he shouted at my retreating back. Not the first time I'd heard the disbelief that a woman could work a crew.

I reached behind my back and tapped the logo between my shoulders, not bothering to turn around. I hoped he didn't think I was being rude or disrespectful. I'd heard bikers could get mad about stuff like that, but I really needed to pee.

The restrooms were one-seaters and someone was already in the ladies' room but thankfully there wasn't a line waiting. I stood outside the locked door, my mind wandering through various work goals for tomorrow, when the noises on the left side of the hallway caught my attention. I looked over to see the men's room door swing open a bit, and got a full-frontal view of the activity going on in there. Stud's pants were down and the black/blue-haired girl was on her knees, rapidly bobbing her head as she sucked him eagerly. I thought the slurping, grunting noises she was making were overkill, but Stud seemed to be enjoying himself. His head was back, and his eyes were closed. One hand was on the top of the girl's head and the other was behind him on the sink to steady him. The girl suddenly shook her head back and forth and growled. Yes, growled! Like a dog with a bone. Or should I say boner.

I slapped a hand over my mouth and stifled a laugh. Somehow

through the loud show, Stud heard me and opened his baby blues to meet my amused gaze. His went wide at being caught getting a blowjob in the men's bathroom and I choked back more laughter. I gave him a "carry-on" gesture along with a thumbs-up and a wink of my own, before reaching for the door and pulling it firmly closed.

The ladies' room opened up and I was able to do my business, wash my hands, and get back to the bar, avoiding the pool-shooting biker as well.

I went to pay my tab and felt a tap on my shoulder. When I turned, my face met a flying hand. Make that a flying hand with claws and a whopping set of sharp rings on each finger. One of them scratched across my bottom lip, drawing a good amount of blood.

"You better stop flirting with my boyfriend, bitch!"

At least that's what I think she said. It was the blonde who grabbed Stud's ass earlier. She was so drunk her words came out more like, "Yoo-beddah schtop furtin wi' mah bowie frenn, bish!" Southern accents were hard enough to decipher, drunk ones even worse.

I raised an eyebrow, giving her a *really?* look while I wiped the blood from my swelling lip with my thumb.

Being the youngest of six, the rest all brothers in a proclaimed Irish family, I was not one to back down from a fight. But however belligerent the woman was, she was weaving back and forth so much that the fight wouldn't be very fair. These were the people my family were working for, and it wouldn't be a good idea to get into a beatdown with one of their women. Besides, I had no idea who she was talking about, Stud or the pool shooter.

"Don't know him or you. I'm just here having a beer and waiting for my brothers," I imparted, hoping she would get the hint and move on. I lifted a finger to my bleeding lip. Damn! That hurt!

Her bleary, wandering eyes finally worked together and focused on me. She looked me up and down and sneered, "Whaddar yoo? One a them lezzbee wimmen?"

My swelling mouth tightened up. This was not the first time I had been questioned about my sexuality. I never cared about anyone thinking I was gay, but I hated it when I got judged on my appearance. I never knew my ma, as she died when I was a baby. I was raised by a pseudo-Irish father who had no clue what to do with a daughter. I worked in my da's company since I was first able to hold a hammer, and growing up he had always treated me like one of the boys. I didn't go dress shopping, I got my brothers' hand-me-downs. When we got haircuts, Da would line us all up at the barbershop and I got the same short do as my brothers (that was one reason I insisted on wearing it long now). I also wasn't small, dainty, and fairy-like. I was around five-foot-eight inches with heavy, muscular shoulders, thick arms, and hard, defined thighs. I was, as they say in the gyms, cut. That happened when you worked a jobsite, lifting, sawing, hammering, drilling, and the rest of the physical work when you're expected to keep up with your brothers. I'd been on this earth for twenty-four years and a good part of that I was pushed to keep up by my brothers and my da.

I reached up and slipped the small silver hoops from my ears. I tucked them into the pocket of my work shirt. If I was going to have to fight, I didn't want to take any chances of having my earlobes torn again. Growing up with five brothers, I was not immune to scraps with them or scraps with other people caused by them. When men fought, they threw punches at the face and gut, and the few times I'd been caught in one of the messes Patrick and Angus started, my male opponent gave up when he realized it was a woman he'd thrown punches at. It was pretty predictable. Women could get vicious, going for the hair and earrings when they fought. They'd grab, pull, slap, and claw at anything they could get to, and they certainly didn't care about the gender of the person they were scrapping with. I was facing the drunk skank and bracing myself. Always best to let them make the first move.

"This is not a good idea. I suggest you move back. Don't start something you can't finish." I hoped my size and low voice would intimidate the skank enough to make her back down. I really didn't want or like to fight. My lip was still bleeding and was starting to burn.

She blinked at my height and thrust her chin out in a show of beer-soaked bravado.

"Ah ain' scairda no man stealin' bish! Yoo think yoo can suckem ov in da back an' me nod find aout?" she declared, waving her hand in front of my face, palm up. I could see that the lethal red nail tips she wore needed new paint. "Ur a goddam freak iz whad yew are! Ah ain' movin! Yew fuckin mooof!"

I sighed. I really needed an interpreter who could speak Southern drunk.

She attempted to place her hands on my shoulders to give me a shove. I blocked her arms easily, knocking them to the sides. She nearly fell over. I rolled my eyes. This was not going to end well.

"BISH!" she yelled, and came at me swinging hard, claws out ready to do some damage. I caught her wrist as it sailed toward my face and used her momentum to knock her to the floor on her knees. I twisted her arm straight back and put a lock on her elbow while she hollered in surprise and pain. Maybe I was going a bit far, but dammit, I was mad! First at my brothers for ditching me here, then at this drunk dumbass, and finally at that man of hers! Had to be Stud since he was the one getting some action in the bathroom.

"I don't know your fucking boyfriend! I'm here in this town to do a job and that's it. Not play around with locals. Not play around with their fuckin' drunk girlfriends. Just a job. Now are you gonna back the fuck off or do I get to finish what you started?"

I finally noticed the silence from both the stage and the bar; the only real sounds were the whispers of the spectators and the drunken whimpering from the blonde I held on the floor. I looked up at Stud, who I assumed started this mess. Apparently he too had finished his business in the bathroom, and he was watching me handle his girlfriend with a fierce scowl on his beautiful face. Stupid cheating bastard! I dropped my eyes from his and looked around. Pool shooter was in the doorway leading to the game room with an amused look. I could see fear on the faces of some bar patrons, speculation on others, and a few sneers of disgust. I closed my eyes and sighed. *Fuck my life!*

"What the hell are you doing, Eva?"

Son of a bitch! Of course my brothers chose that particular moment to show up. I rolled my eyes and dropped the blonde's arm to the floor. She pulled herself up, crying and dripping snot.

Patrick and Angus stood in front of me, both tall, whipcord lean and cut like me. We even shared the same ginger-colored hair.

"How many times have I told you to duck with the punches? *Jesus on a bicycle*, you know better than to let anyone get the drop on ya!" Patrick lectured, rolling his eyes and shaking his head. Angus just laughed and slapped his thighs with both hands. This was prime entertainment for both of them.

Me? I did what any younger sister would do when faced with such devoted brothers. I punched one in the gut and the other in the mouth. I nodded at Pool Shooter and gave the same carry-on gesture to Stud as I had earlier. Then I made my big exit, strutting out the door, head high, shoulders back, and swollen lip still oozing a bit of blood. *Drama. Just how I wanted to end my night.*

CHAPTER TWO

Dawn was just kissing the sky when I stepped out of my tiny house, big cup o' joe in hand and my favorite monster claw fluffy slippers on my feet. It was beautiful up here in the mountains of North Carolina. The sky was striped with color. Blues, grays, reds, oranges, purples. The early summer air was cool and dry but wouldn't stay that way for long. Still, it was a good day for working the job. I looked up at the high mountains newly covered in green, here and there dotted with white and pink dogwood flowers. I could get used to this!

I breathed deeply of the clean-scented air and took a sip of coffee, wincing a little when the cup rim bumped the torn spot on my lip. Dammit, I hoped Patrick and Angus were in a little pain this morning! Hungover would be better. Fergus MacAteer was not only a tough father, he was a tough boss, tougher still on his family crew. No excuses for missing work, ever. I'd endured many torturous hours of teasing and pranking over being sick, dealing with cramps, or whatever else my brothers could come up with. A little payback was nice once in a while.

I went back into my tiny house. I designed it, earned the money for it, built it, and then bought the truck that pulled it from job site to job site. Working with my family was tough but it paid really well. My brothers and father lived in the big RV, sleeping on single bunk beds that were attached to the walls. They were stacked three on each side with curtains that were supposed to provide a little privacy. I was there with them for a number of years as a child, but for obvious reasons that got awkward as I grew up. Da managed to get long-term jobs during the fall and winter so we could go to school, but we transferred often, sometimes in the middle of the year. I went to seventeen different schools but somehow managed to graduate with a diploma. Patrick and Angus also managed diplomas, but Connor, Owen, and Garrett got GEDs on the road. College was not an option, as we were a working family, or at least that's what Da said. I always wished I could've gone, but it just wasn't in the cards for me.

When I was fifteen, Da got two long-term jobs back-to-back at Myrtle Beach that lasted for just over fourteen months. First and only time we ever stayed in one place that long. I loved it! I made some friends and I got to know my teachers for a change. One in particular taught wood shop, Mr. Fuller. He helped me with my house. I told him about living with my brothers, one bathroom, no privacy, and that being a girl, it was getting to be a problem. He introduced me to tiny houses that could be mobile. I spent my school shop time building it with his help. Some of the other guys in the class helped as well once they got over me being the only girl there. My other favorite was Mrs. Castillo, the home ec teacher, who introduced me to the other passion in my life.

Da wasn't happy and wouldn't let me move into it, saying it was safer in the main RV, but I managed to convince him and my brothers it would be in their best interest to let me move what amounted to next door. I began leaving my bras and panties hanging in the small bathroom and over my bunk area to dry. I started putting girly scented shower gels and poufs in the shower closet. I made all of them leave the RV when I was showering or dressing, and if they wouldn't I'd lose my modesty and go full monty in front of them. Talk about awkward! This didn't make me happy either, but a girl's gotta do what a girl's gotta do. I think what finally did it was the feminine stuff. I left the boxes of pads and tampons sitting out, even when I wasn't on my period, and when I was, I complained and groaned loudly at night about cramps regardless of whether I had them or not. It didn't take more than three months into the next job before my brothers were begging Da to let me move out. Da finally agreed.

I loved my tiny house. At first it wasn't much more than a giant box with windows, a space heater, and air mattress. I'd started with scraps from the construction site and other leftover bits. Through the years, I'd work on it when I could with what reclaim items I could find in what time I had. Now my house was really a home. Everything in it was my design with the exception of a beautiful dark cherry wood table that my brother Connor built for me. He inlaid a lighter wood to make a checkerboard pattern on the top, so I had a combination dining-desk-coffee-and-game table. I loved my oldest brother!

I had a bazillion coffee mugs, as every time we went someplace new I bought a cheap tourist mug with the name of the place on it. They hung from secure clip hooks on the low kitchen ceiling. So far, I had yet to move my house and smash any on the hardwood floor (from leftover scrap from a jobsite in Oklahoma).

I was proud of my whole house, having spent so much time putting it together just for me. It wasn't big, but it was enough and it was totally mine. Sometimes it was difficult, like when I had to clear the incinerator toilet or when I ran out of hot solar-heated water, but those challenges didn't stop me from claiming my own space. This was not a want, this was a need.

I spotted Connor emerging from the RV, stretching and

buttoning his green work shirt. Even though he was ten years older than me, he was the brother I was closest to. He was the one who got me through my haphazard school life and managed somehow to make sure I had the credits to graduate with a real diploma. He was also the one my da's the roughest on, which was a shame as he's also the one my da depends on the most to keep the business going. At six feet, he was dark haired, broad chested and shouldered, and heavily muscled. Both of us had our mother's green eyes, but I and the younger set of twins were the only ones who got her light ginger hair and freckles.

Connor waved and walked over to me barefoot. The parking lot wasn't completely paved and we were staying on the gravel side. We usually stayed at the jobsite both for convenience and for security. Betsey had offered us accommodations at the club's campground, but Da thought it was too far away from the site. Our tool truck was expensive and full of top-grade equipment; therefore, we stayed with it.

Connor smiled at my goofy slippers. "Got an extra one of those, *beag deirfiúr?*" He gestured at my coffee mug.

I smiled back at his endearment. "Always for you, *deartháir mór,*" I replied. I shuffled in my monster feet back into my house and allowed him entry. I only let Conner into my personal space. Maybe Garrett or Owen if the ever asked, but Patrick and Angus? Never! Living in the RV had been a constant barrage of short-sheeted bunks, shoelaces tied in impossible knots, and mixed-up hair products all through my teenage years. No way would I ever let them do that to me here. I keep one of the closet drawers locked with a good padlock just in case they did get in my house. My most prized and private possessions were in that drawer.

"No rain yet. Should be a good day. Need to get the frames done and up soon. You have the design for the bar?" he asked as I pulled down a mug and poured in the last bit of coffee from the pot I'd made earlier.

"I have a layout on the computer. Betsey approved it already, but I made a few changes and put in some extras that will make better use of the space. More storage, less waste. She's coming by later to see it."

Connor chuckled and sipped his coffee. "I know you're the expert on wasted space. Tiny houses seem to be a thing these days, both mobile and fixed. Yours would be easy to set on a foundation. Maybe get to stay in one place for a change. Be nice to put down a few roots before we turn gray."

I nodded and sipped at my cup as well, leaving the last bit in the bottom. I never cared for the gritty last mouthful that always seemed to come from a French press. I liked my coffee without extra grounds. I probably should've invested in one of those new coffee machines that had the little pod thingies, but I hadn't gotten around to doing that yet. "It would be nice to be in a fixed place. Someday, I hope Da gets tired of the travel and decides to stay put."

Connor looked at the dregs in his own mug. "Yeah, someday," he intoned almost listlessly. He knew as well as I did that someday was very far off.

I wondered why Connor was still here, running Pub Builders when his heart was elsewhere. We were all grown-ass adults and had skills that could land us work anywhere we chose to be. Connor could make kick-ass custom furniture like nobody's business, but still he was slogging around constructions sites, taking shit from Da, and running his ass off to keep us going. I knew part of it was being the eldest and feeling a responsibility to all of us younger siblings. Now I thought it was more habit, not to mention "family business" was drummed into our heads from the cradle.

Why was I still around? In a nutshell, fear. As brash and bold as I was, I still had a fear of being on my own. I'd spent my entire life around my brothers and being without them was unthinkable, even Patrick and Angus.

"Where is everyone? The sun is up. We're burning daylight. Get your arses out here! We have a lot of ground to cover today."

I rolled my eyes at the familiar bellow of my da. His short, stocky figure appeared, striding quickly across the lot toward the job site.

"Looks like someday isna happenin' today, lass!" Connor quipped in a fake brogue. "Let's get out there and keep the old man happy."

CHAPTER THREE

It was midmorning when he showed up. I was working with Owen on the frames. Owen was like Connor in appearance, but didn't have much to say to me other than "hi," "bye," or "hand me a Phillips head." I was holding the two-by-fours in place and he was wielding the nail gun. We didn't talk much, but we worked well together for the most part. The air compressor was going full throttle but still didn't cover up the low growl of a motorcycle. I glanced at the Harley that pulled into the parking lot.

Owen fired the last nail into the stud. "Gotta reload," he stated and walked off. I rolled my eyes. What a wordsmith! I took out my tape measure and started the next piece.

"Hey, Eva," I heard behind me.

I closed my eyes and sighed. I'd been hoping I wouldn't run into him anytime soon, like, how 'bout never again? I guessed I wasn't going to get my wish.

I turned, putting as blank a look on my face as Owen would have. "Mornin', Stud. What's up today?" My brain instantly remembered the look on his face when I caught him getting sucked off in the bathroom. I heard my inner voice say "that's what she said." It took everything I had to keep my face neutral.

He was dressed in worn blue jeans, black boots, and his club's leather jacket with the fiery dragon on the back. He had taken off the full helmet, which left his hair flattened somewhat, and slipped on a pair of reflective sunglasses. I couldn't see his eyes but he was just as beautiful now as he had been last night on the stage. *Player,* my inner voice reminded me.

"You okay? You got hit pretty hard last night." Even his voice was still beautiful. "You took off before I could check."

I guessed he was going to ignore the black/blue haired chick episode as well. Cool.

I wrinkled my nose and made a brush off gesture.

"I've had worse from my brothers. One little bar bitch isn't going to hurt me." *Oh shit, Eva! That bar bitch is his girlfriend, right? Or maybe not, if he was with the other one. Damn! Now I have a case of foot in mouth!*

His lips rose in that half smile that I was sure made panties drop everywhere. He chuckled. "Yeah, you got her back good. I want to apologize for that. She was out of line and had no business starting trouble."

I sputtered. "Yeah—um—thanks. Sorry I called your girlfriend a bar bitch. She was just a little drunk."

He lifted the mirrored sunglasses from his face and frowned. The blue of his eyes struck me again and my breath caught. He really was one of the beautiful people, and I wasn't immune to it even though I knew better than to go there.

"Nikki is not my girlfriend and she was more than just a little drunk. Plastered off her ass. She wants to be my ol' lady and thinks she has a claim. She hasn't figured out yet that it's never going to happen."

"Hmm." I nodded in acknowledgement. *Okay, blonde bimbo is not his girlfriend. He still may be keeping the other one around. Stop it, Eva! Not your business, just here to work. No ogling the man candy.... Shit, now I'm thinking about him in the bathroom again!*

I shrugged, schooling my thoughts and my face.

"I hope you liked the music. We did a couple of original songs last night in one of the last sets, but you'd already left. Right after you punched out your brothers," he said, taking off his black leather riding gloves. His eyes were intense even though his voice was light and joking and that panty-melting look was on his face. *Blue hair. Growling. Shaking head with a bone. Boner. GAH! Too much! Must escape!*

I ducked my head and pulled out my measuring tape once more, keeping my hands busy and giving myself something to do so I wouldn't burst into peals of laughter. "Yep. They're the younger twins of the family and a major pain in my ass most of the time. I missed the next set since I don't think the bouncer was too keen to have me stick around. He didn't say much, but I caught him giving me the stink eye. Sorry I missed your personal stuff."

I heard him chuckle again. "No problem, babe. The bouncer's name is Mute and he doesn't say much to anyone. You're not banned for life. We're playing again next weekend."

Babe? Really? And was that information or an invitation? Feeling a little awkward, I marked a two-by-four with a carpenter's pencil and stuck the squared-off implement behind my ear. "You got any brothers?" I asked, not knowing what else to say.

He hesitated long enough for me to look up. "My brothers are the club." His voice sounded tight. I almost asked another question, but checked myself. *Nope, not going there, Eva!*

Owen came back over and grunted a greeting before picking up the circular saw and cutting the piece of wood exactly to the length I'd marked. I really liked working with Owen, as he never second-guessed me.

I was trying to figure out what to say to extricate myself and get back to work, but at that moment a shiny red Mustang pulled up and an equally shiny woman climbed out. Jeans, high-heeled boots, dark sunglasses, and all attitude. She strode across the loose gravel lot. I grinned—Betsey was always a welcome sight.

"Hey, darlin'!" she greeted, waving. Her long nails were painted a dark orange color that should have clashed horribly with her dyed red hair, but somehow the woman was able to pull it off. "You got time to show me my new workspace again?" she asked politely, but there was an authority to her that made me think not many people told her no. She was funny, fierce, the reigning queen of the MC, and totally dedicated to the club. I liked her a lot.

"Yeah, I got a different mock-up on my computer." I smiled and let my tape measure snap back in its case. "Owen, you got this?"

My brother grunted and nodded. At six feet tall and two hundred and fifty pounds, most of his communication was as apelike as his appearance. Owen was a workhorse, plain and simple.

Since Owen always seemed to be at a loss for words, I filled the silence by talking about the construction of the new River's Edge bar. "We're following the plans for construction but making adjustments as needed. The framing hasn't changed and neither has the budget. It's in Eastern white pine with an exterior of cedar log siding. Connor found a local supplier that had some really nice knotty pine inside paneling that give the walls an interesting grainy look. It won't be a fully traditional log structure, but this framing and siding allows for wiring, plumbing, and insulation that a straight-up log cabin doesn't." I showed Betsey into the work trailer and pulled up my design on my laptop.

"I really lucked out with the supplier Connor found. He's got the bar tops I like to work with in my bar designs. I used the same knotty pine as the image for the bar top to match the look of the walls, but if you want a nice contrast, bald cypress would be a great choice. I kept the basic L-shape of the original but expanded the floor width to give you a bit more work space." I clicked on the bar top to show what the finished product would look like. "This particular one is coated in a thick baked-on resin that will keep the wood looking new for years. The finish is matte to keep with the rustic look, but I can get a shiny finish if you want. The matte finish doesn't scratch up too much and when it does, it can be buffed out easily. The shiny is harder to maintain with all the elbows, purses, glasses, and whatever else your customers will slap on top."

I clicked on another image. "I also included a Chicago style bar rail. That's the lip you see around the edge. That is a separate installation that you can either do in contrasting or matching wood. I recommend it so any spills are contained on the bar and not leaking on your customers. The drain trough runs the entire bar length and any spilled beer can be wiped down with little splatter on the working side as well."

I kept clicking, showing her the increased shelves, ice machine, keg taps, two deep stainless steel sinks, and my other ideas for her bar. My excitement for the project was starting to show. I really liked

STUD

designing and making stuff. "Most of your customers are here for beer in the bottle and the rest want beer on tap. You said most other sales are hard liquor shots, and only a few tourist people want mixed drinks. You don't go through a huge amount of glassware in a night so instead of a bulky under-the-counter box washer that takes up so much space, I found these light brush washers that take no time at all to use, take up very little space, and are very thorough. Even take off lipstick stains, which the box washers don't do as well."

"I love that idea! Liftin' them big trays of glasses get heavy when you hafta get them in and out of the washer," Betsey stated, looking over my shoulder and placing her taloned hand on one of them. "Biggest use we have is them big beer mugs. I tried them beer glasses but Bruiser is so dang big he ends up droppin' them half the time."

"You really know your stuff." A low male voice vibrated close to my ear over the other shoulder. I jumped a bit as I hadn't realized that Stud had followed us into the work trailer and was also looking at my designs. Sweat broke out on my brow, and I suddenly felt nervous about his approval.

"I like the continuity of using the knotty pine but with a darker wood for the rail. Would a stain work?" he asked, seeming to be genuinely interested.

I all but squeaked back, "Yep, I could do a stain instead of contrasting woods. The grain pattern would look more uniform as well."

Betsey clapped her hands twice and made her decision. "I like it! Let's use a darker walnut color on the rail. Great ideas! I love 'em all!" She fingered my ginger hair. "Darlin', your coloring is gorgeous! What kind do you use?"

I stuttered a bit. "Um—this is just me. I don't color my hair."

"That's your natural color? Lord a'mercy!" She continued to poke at my head. "There's so much of it! You have enough hair for three people. And these curls! Do you have any idea how much money women pay to have hair like that?"

I supposed I should've felt uncomfortable having a virtual stranger mess with me, but I'd noticed Betsey had a habit of mothering everyone around her. It was actually nice to talk to a woman for a change.

"Yeah, it's kind of a pain sometimes, but I don't want to cut it. Maybe tame it a little. I use a lot of leave-in conditioners, but the job site can be rough on it sometimes." I was keenly aware that Stud was still in the room and probably listening. Hair care was probably low on his list of priorities, but for some reason he was sticking around.

"Psalm, the woman that owns the Soap-n-stuff store in town has some homemade conditioners that are fantastic for this kind of hair. Tambre loves her stuff. You'll need to go there sometime. In fact, come on up to the Lair this Sunday afternoon. We're grilling out. The boys will be out and I can introduce you to the other ladies. You need some girl time, being around all this testosterone all day!"

All day? Make that all my life!

She glanced at her watch and kept talking, not even waiting for me to answer. "Well, poop! I gotta run get my grandkids. Sign on whatever we gotta sign for this update, Stud. I can't wait to see the new and improved River's Edge."

With that, the whirlwind that was Betsey left the building. I was surprised a dust cloud didn't follow her.

"I hope I have her energy level when I reach her age. Hell, I wish I had it now!" I declared.

Stud laughed out loud, his parted lips showing strong white teeth. "You and me both, babe."

Again with the babe! My stomach fluttered. What could I say? The man was super-hot and I was not immune to it.

"Eva! Where you be, child?" A deep bellow sounded outside just before my da burst into the work trailer. The gray fuzzy caterpillars that served as his eyebrows pushed together and the number eleven appeared as two deep lines between them. "What's the matter with ya, lass? You're supposed to be working alongside Owen. Get your ass back out there. You shouldn't be in here with a *fireann singil!*"

I didn't know which was worse, my da calling me, his twenty-four-year-old daughter, a child, or chewing me out for being alone with a man. I felt my face flush with embarrassment and for a moment really wanted to hide. But as a MacAteer, it was ingrained in me from the cradle not to back down from a fight. At least Stud didn't speak Gaelic.

"Argh! Keep your pants on, Da!" I yelled back in irritation. "Betsey was here and I was showing her the updates for the bar. Stud's here to take care of the final approval." I stood up and placed my hands on my hips, giving my father as big a stink eye as I could. "I need to place an order for the needed bits."

"Work now, order later," he gruffly instructed, and sat down in the chair I just vacated. "I'm not paying you to be on the phone. Let Connor know. Get on with it, ya *cailín leisciúil*!"

It wasn't the first time my da had called me a lazy girl, but it still hurt. I hazarded a glance at Stud. He was looking at my father with an unreadable expression. I was sure he didn't understand the words my da used, but I did see the muscle in his strong jaw flex.

I bit my lip trying to contain my anger at the dressing down in front of Stud—a client. I called to my Irish bitch, rolled my eyes, and huffed out the door, making as grand an exit as I could. "All right, all right! I'm going!" *Fuck my life! Too much drama!*

***

I nursed my snit during the rest of the day, but working with Owen helped a lot. His silence and steady work pace calmed me down and kept me going. Measure, cut, nail. Measure, cut, nail. Over and over again. Patrick and Angus worked as a team on another wall, and Conner and Garrett worked another. Da supervised, groused, and cursed, checking behind us making sure measurements were correct and the nails were firmly set. It was a long day, but between the six of us, we got the four main walls framed.

I had taken off my work shirt and was just wearing a thin white tank top. The heat and work from the day showed, as sweat had soaked through the fabric and made the head to toe covering of sawdust stick to me. No matter. This was one of my favorite moments, when we attached the ropes and raised the heavy frames into place. Just seeing the main structure being set was magnificent! The building was far from completed, but this was when we got to see what we were truly working on and what the end result would yield. Owen and I were pulling, Patrick and Angus were lifting from the other side, and Connor and Garrett were nailing down the bracing. Da was coaching—or at least that's what he thought he was doing. He was mostly yelling.

"Get it up! Pull harder! Don't let it slip!" He gestured and pointed. "Come on, Owen, put your back into it. Eva, get off your ass!"

My hands were encased in heavy work gloves and the lifting rope was wrapped between them. My arms were taut, and I was breathing hard as I leaned back further, straining to lift the first frame. It came off the ground slowly but smoothly and settled into place, just as planned. Patrick and Angus moved to balance the structure in place. Connor and Garrett hammered the frame and bracing in place, while the other four of us held it. After this one, we had three more to lift. I turned my head and out of the corner of my eye noticed Stud was standing in the doorway of the work trailer. He had spent the day there, at the corner desk working on his computer, a briefcase full of papers beside him, him wearing glasses the whole time. I'd seen him there, clicking away at the keyboard, when I had entered the trailer to take a break and cool off in the air-conditioning. He'd smiled at me every time and had said something friendly or joking, and I had quipped back. Now he was watching the lifting procedure with interest.

"Pull at it harder, Eva!" my father bellowed, breaking into my thoughts.

"That's what *he* said!" Patrick called out, laughing at his own joke.

I rolled my eyes and barked at him, "*Amaideach bodalán!*" Owen and I attached the ropes to the second frame. Da yelled out, "Get it up!" and Angus loudly yelled back, "That's what *she* said!" More laughter rang across the job site.

Both Owen and I were pulling hard at the fourth frame as it lifted off the ground when it happened. Owen's foot slipped, and he fell. The huge frame became unbalanced and was falling back, its weight coming down at an odd angle on top of my brothers who weren't in position to catch it. I was holding back the entire weight of the frame and it almost jerked me off my feet. With a cry, I lay back into the rope, pulling with everything I had in me. I could feel my feet sliding a bit and I set my weight and strength against the massive frame, trying to keep the heavy bulk from slipping back. If it fell, it would either break apart or hurt one of my brothers. My arm muscles bulged with strain, sweat poured from my skin, drenching my tank, and I cried out against the pull in my shoulders. I felt something give, but I couldn't let go.

"Hold it, Eva!" I heard Connor call. I couldn't answer as I was too busy breathing and pulling. Owen got his feet back under him and finally added his strength to mine. Patrick and Angus were able to get under it safely and take more of the weight. The frame lifted into place. Connor and Garrett started firing the nail guns, shooting the heavy nails into the frames and foundation. Braces went up and the basic structure was completed.

Once I could let go, I bent over and took heaving gulps of air. This wasn't the first time I'd held a frame by myself, but it was the biggest and heaviest I'd ever helped to lift, and the few seconds I'd had to hold this one alone had done some damage. Why Fergus had decided to make the frames in single long units instead of three or four shorter ones per wall, I didn't know. I had heard Connor arguing with him over that before the frames were constructed, but it was Fergus's call since he was the boss, and we all had to do as told. I think sometimes he made decisions just to argue with Connor, making sure everyone knew who was in charge, even if Connor was right. Connor usually backed down from the force that was our da, but all of us knew there were times Da was just being stubborn. So far no one had been seriously hurt, but we had had a few close calls. This was one of them.

A dripping wet water bottle appeared under my bent torso. I glanced up, dirty, sweating, red-faced, and puffing, to see Stud standing next to me, cool, drop-dead gorgeous, and breathing normally with his mouth closed. If I'd had the strength, I would have rolled my eyes.

"Thanks," I gasped and took the bottle. I twisted the cap off and took a long swallow, hoping not to choke. The cold was almost painful against my throat.

"You okay?" he asked. "That was a lot of weight to hold. Did you strain something in your back?"

His concern was nice, but noticed. Connor was watching us.

"Nah," I gasped, my breath getting back to normal. I stood up straight even though my back protested the movement. "I'm good. Takes more than a giant piece of wood to lay me out." *Oh shit! Did I really just say that out loud!*

Patrick had sidled up and now slapped me on my back, pitching me forward a bit. "That's what she said!" he crowed. "Nice work, sis! We'll make a man out of you yet!"

I wished he knew how much that statement bothered me.

I retaliated by putting two fingers at the top of the bottle, pointing it at him, and squeezing the middle sharply. A small jet of water shot out, hitting him square in his laughing face. This shut him down temporarily and started Angus roaring with laughter.

"Never will make a man out of her, Patrick! She's got tits! Little ones, at least!" he belted out while grinning from ear to ear and walking up to us, pointing at me.

I looked down at my chest and saw the sweat had plastered my thin sports bra and tank to my skin, leaving nothing to the imagination. I wasn't big chested, but I was rounded and proportioned fairly well. My nipples were even shadowed enough to see and had drawn into tight little buds that were visibly poking out. Stud was right there looking!

I flushed with embarrassment, but since my skin was already reddened from the exertion of lifting the frames, I figured no one could really tell. I covered by taking aim and blasting another stream of water, nailing Angus in the face as well.

Da was across the job site dressing down Owen for slipping. Garrett was shutting down and bleeding out the air lines on the compressor for the nail guns. Connor was putting tools away in the giant rolling chests that were stored in the work van.

"How 'bout you two fucking degenerates go help clear the site so we can get this day over? I'm ready for a shower and a shot!" I declared, tossing the empty bottle at Patrick, standing just past a frowning Stud.

My brother caught it with a big goofy grin and chucked it into the nearest trash bin. "Da put an Irish stew in the pot this morning.

You coming over for a bit?" he asked.

I hesitated. Da was a great cook and his stew was the best. "Yeah, I'll come grab a bowl in a few minutes."

My brothers wandered off, laughing and smiling. The two biggest, happiest men I knew; nothing much affected their perpetually fun-loving natures. They drove me crazy, but it was hard to stay mad at them too long.

I grimaced and grabbed my left shoulder and rotated my arm. It had taken the majority of the weight when Owen slipped. I hadn't felt anything tear, but I knew something had been badly pulled and I would be sore tomorrow. My deltoid twinged as I stretched and massaged it. I felt another hand join mine in kneading the tight muscle.

"You sure you're okay?" Stud spoke softly in my ear. "You may have an injury and just don't feel it yet."

I bit back a groan at the painful yet wonderful dig of his fingers into my shoulder blade. I wasn't sure which I liked more, the feel of my muscle loosening or that it was Stud who was touching me.

"Yeah, I'm good," I repeated, hopefully sounding nonchalant and uncaring. "There's nothing a couple shots of Jameson and a good sleep won't fix. I'll be fine tomorrow. Don't tell my brothers, though. I'll never hear the end of it!"

I was trying to be lighter, but Stud was not amused. "If you're hurt, shouldn't you tell them? They should be concerned. I'm not too keen on them talking about you like that around me either."

Damn, that was unexpected! I'd never had a situation where someone was actually taking up for me against my brothers. I reacted in my typical Eva fashion by throwing it off and laughing. "If I was really hurt they would be, but for the most part, they'd give me a hard time for being—"

I turned to face Stud and wrinkled up my nose. I was covered in sawdust and sweat, my hair dirty and frizzy escaping the sloppy ponytail I'd scraped it into that morning, bruised and sore from various pops, nicks, and other minor hurts on the job, and I probably didn't smell too good right then.

"—a fucking girly girl!" I finished in an Arnold Schwarzenegger voice.

Stud finally loosened up and laughed, shaking his head at me and giving me that crooked smile of his. "Eva, babe."

My stomach curled again.

"Eva!" I heard my da bellow. "Get the lead out and help your brothers. Supper is on soon."

I rolled my eyes and bellowed back, "Keep your pants on, Da, I'm coming."

I waited for it, knowing one of them wouldn't be able to resist. It was Angus this time.

"That's what she said!"

CHAPTER FOUR

I made my way back to my tiny house, full of Da's great lamb stew. I was parked on the opposite side of the lot from the job site, partly because my house had specific needs when setting up, and partly because it gave me a chance for some real privacy from my brothers. Incinerating toilets and other wastewater drains and systems had to be set up and maintained carefully in tiny houses or else there would be unholy messes to deal with later. Privacy was something I grabbed anytime I could.

I listened to the constant shushing sound of the river as it flowed between its wide banks. People always talked about how quiet the mountains were, but I really didn't get it. At night, crickets and other bugs hummed and chirped, and in the morning, birds twittered with their different calls and sounds. Once in a while, the muted roar of a motorcycle could be heard making its way up to the MC's compound, commonly called the Lair. At least the hammering, sawing, buzzing, and banging of the day was gone, as well as the cursing of my brothers and the shouts of my father.

When I got to my house, I immediately took a shower, cleaning the grime and sweat of the day from my body. When I lived in the RV with my family, getting clean daily was sometimes difficult. Seven people use a lot of water and the RV had limited supply. Sometimes we were able to stay at a campground close to the job site, sometimes travel centers, but there were jobs where we had to take care of our own needs. I had built a big shallow box on the roof of my tiny house that functioned as a rain barrel. It had a small solar panel for heating and was attached to a gravity-fed shower. This setup allowed me to take one anytime I wanted. The water was usually hot enough from the solar heater, but once in a while it was cold. Either way, I was able to bathe on a daily basis and not have to endure a time limit, nor the teasing that came with it in the RV. Connor came over from time to time to borrow my shower and I let him, but there was no way I'd extend that offer to my other brothers, especially Patrick or Angus. No telling what kind of nasty funk they would leave behind.

I dried off, wincing at the pull of my abused shoulder, and

rotated my arm in the socket. I hadn't torn anything, but I knew I would be feeling it for several days. Small injuries on the job site were common and very rarely did a day go by that I didn't have some sort of jab, scrape, or bruise. I barely acknowledged them, they were so common. Big injuries happened, but were rare.

I slicked back my hair and combed through some of the leave-in natural conditioner I used, and slathered my body in my favorite sandalwood-scented lotion. This was my time, at night. No brothers around to tease me. It had been weeks since I'd indulged myself, and I was ready. I draped the damp towel over the bar on the back of the bathroom door and shimmied up the ladder to the sleeping loft, the padlock key in my hand, and I unlocked my treasure drawer.

I donned some of my favorite black lacy underwear. Despite being around my brothers for 98 percent of my time, despite working in a male-dominated field, I was still a woman and I liked woman stuff. Lacy, silky underwear that didn't come in a plastic tube was one thing I could indulge in and not get any grief about it from my brothers. I kept my stash in my treasure drawer as well as some other items I didn't want my brothers to know I had. Makeup, stockings, and garter belt, and the only pair of high-heeled shoes I owned, Jimmy Choos I bought on eBay. They had multiple silver straps across the toes dotted with shiny sequins, an ankle strap, and a tall, thin, spiky heel. I had one LBD (little black dress) in my secret girly collection. I'd spent more than one night in my tiny house dressed up and strutting around, pretending to be a sexy lady instead of a working grunt. I was tempted to play with my shoes now, but the way my back felt, I would end up looking like a heron with a broken leg. Instead, I put on my favorite Mickey Mouse lounge pants, another loose black tank, and my fuzzy slippers. My hair was starting to dry and curl despite the conditioner. Maybe a visit to this shop Betsey mentioned earlier would be a good idea.

I moved around somewhat painfully in the main room and pulled up the seat of my built-in sofa, revealing one of my other private treasures. My sewing machine! I'd learned the art of sewing from Mrs. Castillo, my other favorite teacher at Myrtle Beach.

This was my other passion. The one I kept from my family. Connor knew about it only because he caught me one night while I was piecing together the quilt that now lay on my loft bed. Mrs. Castillo was the sewing and design teacher at the school I managed to attend for a whole year. A large Italian woman, she had taken me under her ample wing, teaching me how to design and sew my own clothes and other stuff. I fell in love with the art. Choosing colors, styles, designing and piecing different fabrics together, was something wholly mine that I didn't have to share with my brothers. I'd made a number of my own clothes, including the pants I was wearing. All my handmade clothes were made to fit and flatter my body. I'd made my one LBD from an old pattern I bought at a Goodwill store for a quarter and adapted it to my own body. Why not? It really didn't matter to me whether I needed this type of dress or not. I really liked making something that was truly girly-girl just for me. The fabric was a deep maroon, not black, but since I would never really have a place to wear it other than strutting around my own little space, I didn't think color was an issue. I had never worn it in public because I didn't go to places I could wear it. To my family I was Eva, a hardworking carpenter and their sweaty, cursing, loud, jeans and T-shirt clad little sister who was just another one of the guys. Deep down, I really just wanted to be Eva, woman, strong but soft, dresses, heels, makeup, hair, a woman who had doors opened for her, a woman who was asked to dinner and movies, a woman who was treated like a lady and not another set of working hands.

Maybe someday. Just not today.

I set up my machine on my table, got out the latest project I'd been working on, and put on my radio to an oldies station that had decent reception. Sewing was a good way to wind down from the day. At least I thought so, however my shoulder was really starting to throb and bug me. Keeping it moving around would hopefully bring some of the swelling down and stave off a little of the soreness I'd have tomorrow.

I was running a long seam when a knock on the door made me jump a little and go off track. Earlier Connor had mentioned coming over to my place to shower off the day if the RV was running out of hot water. I knew he also found the place crowded from time to time, and he too needed his space to get away. The jobsite provided electricity through several long hookups so the solar panel had some help, but the water was limited over there.

"Come on in, Connor!" I called out. "Shower is open and there should be enough hot water left!"

I heard the door open and I looked up expecting to see my brother. Instead, I found myself eye-to-eye with the last person I thought would come to my door.

"Monster feet?" a laughing voice asked. "The look goes well with Mickey."

I closed my eyes and nearly groaned. *Fuck my life!*

"Thought you were my brother. Why are you here?" I stood and came around my work table, fuzzy monster feet and all. My house seemed even tinier with him in it. His size, his perfection, his presence overwhelmed my small abode. My heart started to pound and I became hyperaware of him. The feeling was unusual for me, disturbing and a little frightening. No, I wasn't scared of Stud. I was scared of the way I was reacting to him. *Crap! I'm not wearing a bra!*

"Checking on your back and shoulder, babe. I told Betsey 'bout the accident today, and she wanted to send you this stuff. She said it smells like shit and stings like a bitch, but there's nothing better for sore muscles."

He held out a tub of thick white cream. Betsey was right; the stuff reeked.

"I'm good, Stud." I wasn't, but I didn't want to admit it out loud. "I took a hot shower."

He frowned. "Doesn't look like you're good. You're holding yourself funny and standing stiff. You can't be comfortable. I'm sure the shower helped, but this stuff will help more and may make it easier for you to sleep. Turn around and I'll put it on your back. As strong as you are, I'm sure you can't reach that spot between your shoulders."

Sweet Jesus! Is he offering to put his hands on me? On my bare skin? I think I choked a bit.

I took too long in answering. He half smiled and shook his head.

"Come on, Cactus, sit down and relax! I won't bite, I promise. Just let me take care of you." He put a hand on my shoulder, making me sit on my sofa.

"Cactus?" I questioned, trying not to feel the warmth of his skin.

"You're prickly. Cacti are prickly. Therefore, your new road name is Cactus. Here, turn this way."

Well, I couldn't fault his logic. He put his hands on my hips and pulled me to face away from him. I might have wet myself a bit when he moved my hair and draped it over my shoulder. He scooped up some of the smelly cream, and then I felt him dig those wonderful strong fingers into my sore muscle. I hissed at the burn as it made contact with my skin and winced as he dug in.

"Hang in there, babe," he said, keeping the pressure of his hands steady and firm. "Let it sink in."

I couldn't help myself.

"Oh!" I moaned long and closed my eyes in pleasure. "That feels incredible! Mmmmmm!"

I heard a choking sound behind me. I bristled up. "If I hear the words 'that's what she said,' I'm going to turn around and punch you in the nose!"

He laughed out loud again. "Like I said, prickly. No, don't get up. Relax. I got this."

He certainly did.

He kept massaging my shoulder, back, and arm muscles, moving the spaghetti straps of my tank top when needed. My nipples hardened at every brush of the cloth, but since he was behind me, I was sure he couldn't see the reaction. His warm, firm hands felt great, and my soreness grew less and less. I was also getting tight in other places. My nipples hardened into little points and I hoped the black tank was enough to hide them.

"Sewing, eh? Never would have pegged you for a domestic person, but I'm not surprised. You're a very creative woman," he commented.

Thank you, God, for the distraction! Wait? Is this flirting? Is he flirting with me? GAH!

"Thanks," I muttered.

"What are you making?" he asked, his voice going low and breathy. His firm hand kneaded my flesh.

"Umm—just a lap quilt." I let my head droop forward. No

wonder women flocked to him. His hands were magic!

"You make the quilt here on your sofa?" His breath whispered across my neck and I had to stifle a shiver.

"Mm-hmm." I kept my mouth closed to keep from drooling. "Cushions too."

"They're really nice. I think Molly does a lot of sewing and custom work. You'll get to meet her Sunday at the club pool. You've got a lot of movies. *James Bond? Star Trek?*"

"Sean Connery is the best one, hands down. Captain Kirk all the way," I muttered.

I was in heaven. My shoulder and back were relaxed and loose. The smell and burn of the cream wasn't too bad now that it had been worked into my skin. I wanted to relax even further, lean back into that hard body of his, feel his heat behind me—

"Stuuuuuuuud!" a high female voice screeched outside my house.

I jumped three feet in the air, and I think Stud did too. If I hadn't known any better, I'd have thought he forgot he had other company.

"Stuuuuuuuud! How much longerrrrrrr?" Now the voice was imitating a whiny five-year-old.

"Hold up, Bambi. Just a minute," Stud called, his voice sounding normal again.

What the fuck? I could kick myself for thinking he was flirting with me and that his concern for me was genuine. Time to get the Irish bitch out.

I turned to him and raised an eyebrow. "Bambi?" I said with as much derision as I could fit in one word. "Really?"

"I'm just her ride to the Lair tonight, Cactus," he said, laughing at my tone like he found it amusing. Clearly, I needed to work on my Irish bitch.

Yep, I'm sure he's her ride, all right. I rolled my eyes and stood up, breaking contact with his hands. My shoulders felt cold without his touch.

"Yeah, well, I think I'm good now, so you're free to take Bambi to your clubhouse." I stretched long and high, my arms over my head, relishing the renewed feeling in my back. I heard a choking sound come from Stud and I immediately dropped my arms, realizing what kind of show I was presenting to him. "Umm—thanks. I really do appreciate it. I don't usually have anyone do this sort of thing for me. If you ever need a new career, masseur would work. You have my recommendation."

"No problem, Eva. Damsels in distress are my thing," he coughed out as he got up. His eyes met mine and I wanted nothing more than to be lost in their blue. He gave me what was fast becoming my favorite of his expressions, that half smile.

"See you tomorrow, Stud," I answered, watching him turn to leave. "Hey, Stud?" I asked as he opened the outside door. He turned back and looked at me in question. I took a breath. "My family doesn't know about—well… what I do outside of the carpentry and job site work, and—um, I don't really want them to know. Connor is the only one who has seen my sewing, but my other brothers and my da? They just wouldn't get it and I'd have to listen to their shit, so would you please keep my hobby to yourself?"

"No problem, Cactus. I understand. What are friends for?" He chuckled a bit. I was soooo glad he found me amusing.

"Well, friend, some of us can't party all night and have to get up at o-dark-thirty to deal with large and loud power tools. And I'm not talking about table saws and drills!" I quipped, hoping he got the reference to my brothers. Time to put some humor in and lighten up a bit.

It worked. He threw back his head and laughed loudly. "No doubt, Cactus! No doubt!"

"Stuuuuuuuuud!" The whine was back.

His eyes went soft, and he reached out to tap me on the chin with his finger. "Babe, I'm really just her ride to the Lair."

"Well, you'd better get going before she decides to run off with Thumper," I joked while I moved to get back to my sewing. I wanted to redo the crooked seam before I went to bed.

He laughed again as he finally left, seeming to drag his feet. I locked the door behind him and a few minutes later, I heard the distant sound of his bike starting and fading as he left the job site.

I got out my seam ripper and started taking out the tiny stitches.

"Friends. I can do friends."

***

Stud tossed a tequila shot in his mouth and tilted his head back, feeling the burn slide down his throat. The Lair was full of sound and people, a cacophony of music, talking, laughter, and games. This was a typical night at the clubhouse. He spotted Kat behind the bar, serving drinks, still in her nurse's scrubs from her day job at the hospital. Mute, her old man, was nearby as always, watching the crowd for potential trouble. They were engaged and would be married in the early fall, a big biker wedding planned à la Betsey. That woman did nothing by half measures and the club was bearing the expense. No matter. The club was solid both in brotherhood and financially. Besides that, Mute and Kat were perfect for each other. After the obstacles they had faced in their lives, they both deserved some happiness. Stud had no problem writing the checks that were paying for the elaborate ceremony. All the bookkeeping problems had been resolved and Stud was now looking at more investment properties. Maybe another campground or a motel. There was still a lot of work to be done and a lot of papers to be filed, but there was this new place close to Maggie Valley that looked promising.

"Wooo!" A shrill voice screeched in his ear. "I'm sooooooo drunk!" Bambi hung her slight weight on his shoulder and giggled at him, her eyes slightly crossed from the amount of booze she had consumed.

Stud jumped at the sudden noise, irritated at the interruption to his thoughts, but turned and smiled at the staggering girl.

"Is that right?" he crooned, putting an arm around her waist to keep her from falling over. "You wanna slow down a bit?"

She blinked at him. "Huh?"

"Don't you think you've had enough?"

She looked confused. "Had enuff what?"

Stud nearly rolled his eyes. At one time he would have found her drunken cuteness appealing. Now it was more annoying. "Alcohol, sweetheart."

She looked at him owlishly before bursting into a loud cackle.

"Oh Schtud! Yoo zound like mah dad! Yoo'wanna be mah daddy?" she purred, and giggled again, rubbing her barely clad breasts against his ribs and sliding her hand low across his stomach. In her mind, Stud guessed she thought she was being sexy and seductive. In reality, she looked like a drunk kid playing at being an adult. Not the turn-on he needed or wanted at that time. Rather than turn her down completely or hurt her feelings, he gently disengaged himself from her grasp and murmured something about later or another time. She collapsed into a nearby chair whooping and laughing.

Stud grabbed a cold bottle of beer and walked out of the Lair to the upper balcony deck overlooking the high bluff. Below, he could see the river, its calm currents glistening in the moonlight. There were a few lights dotting the opposite bank and below the bluff where the new River's Edge Bar was being built. The party noise was muted slightly but still in contrast to the serene scene in front of him. He tilted the bottle back and took a long drink. A lone light caught his attention from the area outside the work site. Eva was still up, working at her very unexpected hobby. In his mind's eye, he imagined her sitting in front of her sewing machine, stitching away while a movie played in the background. Very domestic and totally opposite of what she appeared to be. He'd never met a woman like her before. She looked like what a fabled Amazonian would: tall, warrior-like, strong, and more than anything else, confident in herself and her surroundings. She knew her craft. Both of them, in fact, and knew them well. He was impressed and intrigued with the redheaded Amazon. Not his type at all and yet he found himself genuinely curious and attracted to her.

A sharp drunken laugh cut through his thoughts, bringing him back to the party going on behind him. He turned to see three hangarounds surrounding the young Bambi like true predators. She was arching her back and grinding her hips, blithely unaware of what she looked like: fresh meat. Stud knew the men around her to be pretty good, and two were being considered as prospects, but at the moment they looked more like jackals ready to pounce. Bambi looked ready for them as well, but there was no way she was ready to take on three of them.

Stud sighed. *I'm getting too old for this.* He swallowed the dregs of his beer and went back into the lodge to rescue the naïve young woman. He stopped in front of the couch where Bambi was sitting. It took her a few seconds to focus on his outstretched hand before she tried her best seductive smile again. Three hangarounds were no match for a full-patched member. She got up and grabbed at his hand, nearly falling because of her ridiculously high stilettos. She awkwardly trotted after him as he led her down the hallway to his club room, giggling and weaving, almost pulling him down. Stud felt like sighing again. When did sex become a duty? Not that he minded it, but he already knew the outcome. He'd fuck the drunken girl, and she would take that as a sign he wanted more than a night's entertainment. She'd end up getting hurt and Stud could add yet another broken heart to his bedpost.

CHAPTER FIVE

"**I**t's straight!" **I yelled down** from my perch at the top of the ladder as I held a long level against the main ceiling joist. "Bubble is directly in the middle." Owen and Garrett were manning the nail guns at either end of the roof frames and I was double-checking the positions, level, and angles of the triangular pre-builds. This was critical to the open ceiling look the interior of the building would have, and each set had to be exact.

"Check it again, girl!" my da yelled back up. "Can't afford any more screw-ups!"

I rolled my eyes. I hadn't screwed up any measurement yet, so I wasn't sure what previous screw-up he was referring to.

"Don't roll your eyes at me, *cailín leisciúil*! Get your ass movin'!"

Shit! He could always tell.

I wiped the sweat from my brow, smearing another layer of dirt on my forehead. We were supposed to wear hard hats on the job site, but we weren't today as no one wanted to deal with the hot, heavy headwear. OSHA would not be happy with us, and if we got caught, they would shut us down in a heartbeat. I wore mine for most of the morning but when the sweat kept dripping into my eyes, blurring my vision, I decided to take a chance.

I spotted Stud coming out of the air-conditioned work trailer. He was wearing his nerd glasses—as I had called them to his face—and was sipping on a cold bottle of water. The bandana around my head was soaking wet and I'm sure my ponytail was dripping as well. I wanted to punch him.

"Yo, Stud! Throw one of those up here! I'm dry as hell!" I called out.

He disappeared briefly inside the trailer and brought out a fresh bottle. Walking toward where I was perched on the ladder, he answered, "Looks like you're wet enough, Cactus."

"That's what she said!" Garrett hollered across the work area. Gah, my fucking brothers! If I had something I could have thrown at him, I would have.

"Can't you find something new, smartass?" I hollered back while coming down from the ladder.

"Do they ever give you a break?" Stud asked, sounding irritated.

He handed me the dripping bottle. He really didn't like the way my brothers talked to me sometimes, even though I'd reminded him more than once that's just the way they were and I was used to it.

"What do you think?" I answered, placing the cold bottle under my chin and rubbing it to the back of my neck.

It was late morning on Sunday and we had been working the site since just before dawn in what was essentially overtime, mainly because Fergus had rented the lifting crane on the wrong dates and we had limited time to use the heavy piece of machinery to lift the pre-builds for the roof framing. This did not fill me with joy as even though we were well over forty hours this week, closer to seventy, my da didn't pay out overtime. I was glad no one lived too close as they wouldn't be filled with joy either at being awakened by the earsplitting sound of grinding machinery. Stud had joined us after he drove by the site and saw us hard at work. To say the least, he wasn't happy we were on the site, but begrudgingly understood why.

It had been several weeks since he came by my house to bring me that fantastic cream and treat me to a rubdown I wouldn't soon forget. I hadn't seen him with bike bunny Bambi again. But then again, he hadn't had much time for her, since he'd started coming over to my place several nights a week to watch movies. The night after Bambi's ride, I got a knock at my door again. Stud had strolled in with a pizza and a six-pack.

"You eaten yet, Cactus?" he'd asked, setting the pizza on my table and lifting a Wicked Weed beer from the cardboard holder. Asheville wasn't too far away from Bryson City, and there were some killer microbreweries there.

"Nope," I'd said, feeling a little confused as to why he was there. "Why are you here?"

"Pizza, beer, and Roger Moore," he'd stated, opening the flat box and picking up a slice of the steaming food. The rich tomato and spice scent hit my nostrils and I caved. Someone bringing food was preferable to going over to my family's place. Da had been in rare form that day, yelling and griping at everything and everyone, and I'd just as soon not deal with him again that night.

"I hope you didn't put anchovies or pineapple on that," I had declared testily, trying to act nonchalant about him showing up at my place at that hour. "Pineapple should be in sweets and cakes, and little fishes on pizza is just wrong."

He laughed. I really liked looking at him when he laughed.

"Not at all, Cactus. Just plain pepperoni tonight. Let me know what else you like, and I'll bring it next time."

I wasn't sure what was worse, him telling me he'd bring me my pizza preference or the fact that he planned on coming to see me again. Then it hit me.

"You're hiding," I crowed with a smile.

He nearly choked on a swallow of beer. "What? Hiding? How the hell did you come up with that?"

I rolled my eyes and plopped down on my sofa with the remote in one hand and a fat slice in the other. "Oh come on, Stud! You've had more women come see you at the job site than I have tourist mugs. You're coming here to get a break from them."

He looked at me funny. "Maybe I do want a break."

Something about his tone sent a warning shiver down my spine, but it didn't last any longer than it took him to pop one of my movies in the DVD player and then flop down next to me. Mmmmmm, he smelled good! Old Spice or Axe or some other good-smelling male stuff.

The opening scenes to *Moonraker* came on and I settled in to watch. Not my favorite James Bond, but not the worst either. I tried to stay awake but long days of physical work didn't make for long movie nights. I drifted in and out for a bit, but at some point dropped off completely. I came back to full awareness right when the credits were rolling. Somehow we had ended up with Stud leaning back into the sofa and me draped halfway over his lap. His arm was around my shoulders with my head on his chest tucked under his chin. His fingers were softly stroking my ribs, just under my breast. I could feel his heat surround me as well as that masculine scent I liked so much. I both froze in place and nearly bolted from it at the same time.

"Please tell me I didn't snore or drool on you," I had implored in as normal a tone as I could. I needed to break the awkwardness of finding myself this close to him and the best I figured was to be

Hard Hat Eva. Irish Bitch Eva wasn't right and he'd already seen that side of me.

He'd burst into laughter and I'd shifted off him, shaking my head and running my hands over my explosion of bed hair. He squeezed me once and lifted his arms, letting me sit up.

"Sorry about falling asleep on you. Long days, you know," I'd muttered, hoping I sounded nonchalant and normal when I was very aware I wasn't wearing a bra and my nipples were hard and pointed. Stud didn't seem to notice. I was sure he'd seen plenty of pointy nipples and one more set wouldn't be a big deal.

"No problem, Cactus. A little drool never hurt anyone."

My eyes had then darted to his in fear and embarrassment, but when I saw the teasing light in them, I groaned and playfully punched his shoulder.

"Smartass!" I growled.

He laughed and stood up. "I noticed you have Netflix. Can you get a signal here?"

"Spotty. Couple of private signals but we're too far away from any real coverage," I said, standing up and stretching. His eyes dropped to my chest and I cringed a little, remembering my pointiness. "It's not like I don't have stuff to do in the evenings. I don't miss it—much."

"Ever seen *House of Cards* on there?" he asked, gathering the empty pizza box.

"Yep. One of my favorites. Waiting for the new season to come out," I answered.

"It's out now," he said, grinning.

"Damn! I'm missing it!" I lamented. It really was one of my favorite series and even better, I didn't have to wait week to week to see a new episode. I did binge watch from time to time when I was able to. Didn't happen often unless there was a rain deluge and work at whatever site was impossible.

He nodded. "I have band practice tomorrow night, but I'll come Thursday and bring food. We can get in one or two episodes if you can stay awake long enough."

He wasn't asking. He was telling, but I could still say no.

"Sure, sounds good." *Holy shit! Was this a date? Did he just make a date with me? Argh!*

He sauntered in his Stud way to the door and opened it, still carrying the pizza box.

"Gotta work on that snoring, Eva. I thought the roof was gonna cave in at one point." He grinned as he turned in the open door and gave that parting shot.

My mouth gaped open and my eyes went wide. I picked up a pillow from the sofa and threw it at his head.

"Smartass!" I shouted again as he closed the door against my missile. I could hear him laughing as he fired up his bike and left.

Netflix and food on Thursday night with Stud. Fuck my life!

True enough, Stud had showed on Thursday night, this time

with Chinese food. I wasn't picky, especially when I didn't have to cook. He also brought some sort of device thingy that boosted the spotty Wi-Fi for the bar's signal. Netflix came in clear and we settled in for a night of political and character debate on the series. I didn't fall asleep this time, mainly because of the lively conversation and endless teasing.

This past week he'd been out to my place every night. He was becoming a comfortable but confusing habit. A habit I didn't want to quit but one I didn't know what to do about. Connor had asked me about the sound of the Harley motorcycle coming to my place so often but didn't give me any shit about it. Da could sleep through Armageddon and never noticed. If my other brothers knew about the visits, they were minding their own business for a change.

Betsey's Mustang rolled into the lot, top down and blaring an Aerosmith song. She slipped out of it on her heeled boots and tight distressed jeans. Her two grandchildren were bouncing in the back seat.

"Stud!" she called. "Brick's called for a church meet at noon. I got the kids and we're doing a grill-out on the fly. The prospects are setting up, but I need some stuff from Costco and you still got my card. Hey, Eva!"

How she got all that out in one breath, I didn't know. I poured the last of my water down my throat.

"Hey yourself, Betsey." I waved.

"You look plumb tuckered, child!" she exclaimed as she made

her way over to where Stud and I stood. "Come on up to the Lair as soon as you can. We got plenty of food and I bet the pool will feel real good on a day like today. You bunch been workin' nonstop since you got here. Time to take a breather."

Da and Conner came up.

"Well, Ms. Davis, I'm not sure about that," Da started, shaking his head. No one could ever call him a social butterfly. His life chiefly consisted of work, more work, traveling for work, and occasionally sleeping.

"Pshhht!" exploded from Betsey's red painted lips. "Nonsense, Fergus! All y'all come up. Ain't nothing better than a summer party. The boys have that church meeting, but there ain't much to talk about as far as I know." She snatched the white Costco card from Stud's outstretched hand. "Y'all got swimsuits?" she asked. "Don't matter none. Most of the boys just wear cutoffs anyway, and I'm sure you got some somewhere. *Michelle! Quit jumping on my seats and sit your butt back down!* How 'bout you, darlin'?"

It took me a moment before I realized she was talking to me and not the squirming child in the back of her car. "Yes, ma'am, I have one," I replied, thinking of the bikini I made for myself last summer.

"Lord a'mercy, darlin', I ain't no ma'am. I'm just Betsey to everyone round here. Anyway, it *is* Sunday and we got us a date at the pool, remember? All y'all come up! Don't you get some time off on the Sabbath?"

Fergus grumbled a bit but nodded. Connor spoke, "We're ahead of schedule and at a good stopping place for the day. Thank you, Betsey, we'll be glad to come up to the Lair. It would be a glorious break, and I think we all need it."

"Fantastic! Come on up in about an hour. Just bring yourselves and an appetite. *Cody! Imma gonna spank your behind if ya poked another hole in my headrest! Put that pencil away!* I love my grandkids to death but they're 'bout to drive me crazy! I hope I can get 'em tired enough in the pool so they'll sleep tonight. Their mama and daddy are going through a nasty divorce right now and it ain't pretty at all! I gotta run. See y'all later!" She got into her car and waved as she drove off.

Da and Connor looked stunned, as if they just got hit by a wild storm. They finally wandered off toward my other four brothers, who were still working the site, to share the spur-of-the-moment invitation.

I stood holding my empty water bottle, still trying to make sense of her smiling and speaking to us in a friendly Southern voice and in the next moment yelling like a banshee at her grandkids. I turned to Stud with a slightly stunned expression on my face.

"Did that just happen?"

Stud grinned and slapped a hand on my shoulder. "Yep. That's hurricane Betsey. Best mother hen you'll find anywhere on the planet."

I grinned a sweaty grin back at him. "I think I'm a little scared of her."

STUD

He laughed out loud. "Yeah, me too. Listen, I have a couple items to finish up. How 'bout if you go get your stuff together, get cleaned up a bit, and I'll give you a ride on my bike. Bring regular clothes in case you want to change later. Yeah?"

I blinked. "Never been on a bike before that I didn't power with my own two feet on a set of pedals."

It was Stud's turn to blink. "Never?"

I shook my head. "Nope." I said popping the *p* a bit.

He smiled what I had dubbed his devil smile. "Oh, Cactus! You're in for a treat!"

CHAPTER SIX

I blew through a shower, washing the sweat and dust from my body and hair, and took a little time to shave my pits, legs, and bikini line. I jammed underwear and a sports bra into my backpack, thinking the clothes I would put on to ride in would be clean enough to change into later, and added my hairbrush and an elastic hair tie. I put on my purple bikini, looked in the mirror, and almost took it off again. I'd made the suit for those occasions I got to lie in the sun and tan. No one had seen it but me, and there was a lot of me showing. I shrugged off the intimidated feeling and kept it on since I didn't have anything else I could wear. There was no way I was missing a chance to dip in a pool. I didn't bother with makeup as I knew it wouldn't last. I threw on a pair of shorts and a company T-shirt, as that was the last one I had that was clean. *Damn! Time to make a trip to the laundromat.*

Stud was waiting for me outside my tiny house. I saw Connor watching us as he waited for my other brothers to get themselves sorted. He had a frown on his face, but I didn't bother to wait around and ask him what was up his ass. I was too excited about getting to ride on a motorcycle.

"Okay, Stud, how do I do this?" I asked, bouncing a little. I slung the backpack over my shoulder and he handed me a helmet, which I crammed on my still wet head.

"Is this your only one? What are you gonna wear?" I asked while buckling the straps under my chin.

He smiled. "I don't have another one with me, but this isn't a real ride. Barely a couple miles up the hill. I'll take you for a real ride sometime on the Tail."

I'd heard about the famed stretch of road called the Tail of the Dragon. Full of tight twists and turns, it was supposed to be a biker's wet dream. I grinned at him.

"You're on, pal! Let's blow this joint! I gotta date with a pool and you're holding me up!" Did I mention I loved swimming?

He laughed at me and pointed out the pegs where I would put my feet. I managed to mount behind him and not groan at feeling his body so close to mine. My knees were spread around his hips and I lightly grasped his waist. He grabbed my wrists and pulled me closer, placing my hands on his hard stomach. It took all my super control powers not to feel him up a bit. I didn't have to resist long, as with a roar we were off and shooting out of the lot.

He was right. Even though the ride was a short one, just up to the much-talked-about Lair, I loved it!

I squealed and clutched him harder when he revved the engine and opened up the throttle. Shit, I was being such a girl, but I didn't really care. The big red and chrome machine rumbled under me as if it were alive. I leaned when Stud leaned, feeling the movement and power of the bike as it pulled around the turns. I could feel him smoothly changing gears.

All too soon the ride was over and we arrived at the Lair. It looked more like a camping lodge resort than an MC clubhouse, but I wasn't going to complain. I got off the bike first, swinging my leg high enough to make sure I didn't get tangled and end up on my ass. Stud backed into a spot along a row of fancy bikes. I didn't know enough about them to tell one kind from another, but I decided I would be doing some serious googling very soon.

"That was amazing! I want a bike!" I crowed after Stud shut down his bike and joined me.

He laughed again, totally amused.

"I'm serious! I'll have to get a trailer or something to hook up behind my house, but I'm definitely getting one! How hard is it to learn how to ride? Do you have to have a special license?" I peppered him with questions as he led us around the lodge to the back area where the sounds of music and happy screaming children could be heard.

He kept laughing and shook his head. "Too much, Cactus! Grab a spot close to Betsey and the other old ladies." He pointed to a trio of women lying in lounge chairs close to the pool's edge. "The one on the right is Molly, Cutter's woman, and the other one is Tambre, Taz's woman. You'll meet the other members later, after church. Speaking of which, I need to get going. You gonna be okay?"

I looked in his eyes. I couldn't say I wasn't intimidated a bit by being left by myself in the midst of a bunch of strangers, especially women, but I was a MacAteer and could brazen out anything. Hell, I'd been in bars far more dangerous than this.

"Go pray, confess, or whatever else you do in church. I'm gonna get wet!" I declared.

Stud snickered, and I gave him the best evil eye I had. "Don't say it!" I threatened, balling up my fist and shaking it at him.

He threw back his head and let out a roar of laughter. I loved it when he did this with me. Friend zone or not, I loved making him laugh, seeing his eyes glow and the sounds of his pure mirth. He wrapped a hand around my neck and pulled me in closer. I wasn't expecting what happened next, and I had no idea how to handle it.

He kissed me.

Not just kissed me, but *kissed* me!

His lips covered mine and he drew me in. I lost my breath somewhere. His tongue traced my mouth and I felt a zing straight through my breasts to between my legs. I opened up, mostly in shock, and he dove right in. It was powerful. It was wet. It was wonderful. It was—Holy shit! I panicked.

I'd snuck a few kisses once or twice with a boy I liked in my Myrtle Beach high school year. He told me he liked me as well, but when you're a girl with five older brothers and a tough as nails father, it does not make for easy romantic relationships. Fergus nixed that budding romance quickly and thoroughly—when the boy showed up for the one single date I had, all six of my male family members stood around the poor teen in a circle and grilled him on where we were going, when we'd be back, and "don't you dare think we won't find you if you do something we don't like."

"What the fuck do you think you're doing?" I gasped, pulling away, grabbing at my inner Irish bitch and bringing her out. She was my automatic defense anytime I got panicked or scared. On the outside, she could deflect nuclear missiles. Inside, I was shaking like a leaf, wondering if my breath was okay and wishing he would do it again.

"Help me out, Eva, please play along," he whispered low against my mouth. About that time I heard a vaguely familiar whine.

"Stuuuuuuudly!"

I turned to Bike Bunny Bambi. She was younger than I'd

thought she would be, barely in her twenties, with short dark hair, brown eyes, and a pouting mouth. She didn't have a lot up top but what she did have was popping out of a tiny yellow bikini top. I was guessing her short shorts covered a matching bottom.

Ah, I get it now! He just wanted an out and I was convenient. I put away the bitch, but strangely, couldn't decide between relief or disappointment.

Stud spoke to the visibly upset girl. "Bambi, I'm with someone else tonight. I told you how it was earlier this week."

"But I thought we were gonna hook up?" She stuck out her lower lip. It was probably supposed to make her look cute and appealing, but instead it made her look like a belligerent child gearing up for a big tantrum.

Actress Eva to the rescue.

"Sorry, Bambi," I found myself saying in a squeaky voice. I wrapped my arms around Stud's neck and snuggled close. *Snuggled!*

I had to admit it was nice. Especially when he put his arm around my waist and pulled me closer.

"He's *my* hookup tonight." I put as much saccharine sweetness into a breathy voice as I could. Totally not me. *Gag!*

"You can have him again next week. Tuesday is open." I widened my eyes and squealed. "Ooooooh! I know! I just had the best idea! We can take turns! You know? Like on a rotation schedule! Ooooh! I'm sure the others will like it too!"

His hand tightened at my waist, probably warning me I was going too far. *Deal with it, buddy. You asked for this.*

"Others?" she asked, her light bulb dimly lit. "You mean he's got more than one hookup?"

It took everything I had not to burst out laughing. Instead I nodded sagely.

"Uh-huh! There's lots and lots. Like a whole harem!" I giggled and curled a lock of Stud's hair around my finger while his eyes showed both irritation and amusement. "We all share Mr. Studly Muffin."

He squeezed my waist hard enough to make me jump. Apparently "Mr. Studly Muffin" was too much. I ignored him.

I turned back to the girl. "But it would be sooooooo much better if we all like, you know, had a schedule or something? Like a calendar to, you know, like sign up for a time slot or something? We should, like, totally put one up and everyone can like, you know, sign their name for a regular night."

The girl was still not getting it. "You mean, like, I gotta wait my turn?"

I smiled a big vacant smile. "Yeah! Like that! So awesome, doncha think?"

"Eva," Stud warned, clearly not amused anymore. His hand at my waist squeezed again, and I ignored it again.

"I dunno." The girl looked like her brain needed some serious oiling. The gears were grinding slowly and a breakdown was imminent.

"Well, it's my turn tonight!" I turned back to Stud and pouted, sticking out my lower lip in a perfect impression of Bike Bunny Bambi. "You need to get to your meeting, sweetie pook. I'll see you at the pool later." I pecked him quickly on the lips, keeping in character, and walked off toward the sounds of splashing and screaming children. "Bye, Studly Muffin!" I called. I think he growled.

The look he gave me as I made my grand exit promised retribution. Okay, maybe I did take it a bit too far, but damn, that was fun!

CHAPTER SEVEN

The in-ground pool itself wasn't much more than a hotel size unit, but the surrounding deck was beautiful. The lip of the pool was tiled in blues, grays, and greens, and the wooden deck around it was stained in a deep redwood. There were tables off to the side covered with food, and a small picnic shelter a little further out. I could see another biker manning a huge grill. He wore a leather vest I'd seen on all the club members. They called it a cut. This one didn't have all the patches on it—called rockers. He must still be a prospect and hadn't quite earned a membership yet.

I made my way over to Betsey and her friends.

"Hey, girlfriend!" Betsey greeted me from her lounge chair and gestured to the two ladies on her right. "This is Molly, and that's Tambre. I think you met them at the temp bar in town a few weeks ago but didn't really get introduced."

She turned her head to her companions. "This here's Eva. She's one of the construction people working on the new bar."

Molly perked up. "Hey, Eva! Stud told me about you! Nice to finally meet you, girl!"

What? Wait! Stud talked to her about me? Probably my sewing. What did he say? Grrr! I was so going to tape a Studly Muffin sign-up sheet somewhere in the clubhouse.

"Hey, Eva. You want a drink?" Tambre said in a soft, friendly alto as she got up from her lounger. "Only sweet tea right now, I'm afraid. Too many kids are in the pool. Betsey will mix up margaritas later."

"Grab a lounge and sit yourself down. I can't believe you were workin' this mornin'! I heard that crane all the way up here," Betsey commented, smearing some sunscreen on her skin.

"Fergus rented the crane and messed up on the dates. The company's coming for it tomorrow, so we had to get the roof frames lifted and in place today. Good news is we're ahead of schedule. Bad news is there's a big rain forecasted for Tuesday and Wednesday next week that may put us behind." I set my small backpack down and began stripping off my clothes. I had my swimsuit on underneath, but I still felt funny dropping my shorts in front of people.

"Damn, girl!" Molly exclaimed. "That's some serious Amazon

shit you got going on! No wonder you kicked Nikki's ass so easily."

Huh? I looked at her in surprise.

"Yeah, darlin', we heard about the bar fight with Nikki," Betsey added casually while stretching out with a big pair of sunglasses perched on her nose. "That girl needed her ass kicked. She's been chasin' Stud forever, tryin' to be his old lady. She ain't gotta clue yet, he's not old man material. Not with his experience."

Tambre came back and handed me a tall sweating glass of amber liquid. I took a long drink. *Oh yeah! Nothing like ice-cold Southern sweet tea! Champagne of the south!*

"He's got some other chickie chasing him now," Tambre mentioned as she pulled up a lounger for me to use.

I nearly choked. "Sorry," I gasped and thumped my chest. "Wrong pipe."

"Yeah, I heard. Some girl that waitresses over at that new Mexican place. Great food. Calls herself Bambi." Betsey kept her eyes on the kids splashing around in the pool. "She's here today but probably gone tomorrow. You know how Stud is."

I nearly sighed in relief.

"They had a hookup a while back, and she's been angling for another one ever since."

I nearly gagged.

"He's rode her around a few times on his bike, being the gentleman he is, but she ain't figured it out yet. He ain't interested and ain't gonna be interested."

I coughed.

Molly sighed and shook her head. "Pity. He's such a good man and we all know there ain't too many of them out there." She turned to me. "It's really his people back in Raleigh, you know."

"Amen, sister!" Betsey declared.

I was feeling very out of my element. Girl talk was something I rarely experienced.

"Um... he's from Raleigh?" I stuttered.

Betsey took a big sip of her drink and gestured before continuing. "Mmmm—yes, darlin'. He's one of a kind. He comes from what they call 'old money,' and he's got a lot of it. Family is loaded. Big name and good ol' boy law firm his people have had for generations. Stud was on his way up that ladder with his fancy law degree and a big ol' trust fund. Lord a'mercy, he had it all! Then something happened and he turned his back on it. Left it all behind him. He came out this way 'bout eight years ago and stopped at the bar for a drink. Talked with my husband, Brick, just about all night and got hisself invited to the Lair. This was before we had all the stuff we have now. I don't even think all the cabins at the campground were up yet. Remember, Tambre?"

The older woman nodded sagely and muttered, "Sure do."

Betsey paused for another sip of tea. I took another one as well, dying to hear more.

"Anyway, Stud decided to stick around that summer. Helped us set up the accounting books, get the numbers straight, and things of that nature. He's real good with that stuff. Brick prospected him and patched him in pretty quick. Been with us ever since. I tell you, there ain't no one more loyal to the club than him, but what happened to make him turn his back on his people in Raleigh messed him up. As good as he treats his women, he ain't never gonna be real with just one. It's a damn shame. He's such a good man."

"What happened?" I tried not to sound interested, even though I was bursting with curiosity.

"I'm thinkin' it's somethin' to do with a woman," Molly chimed in. "He ain't never been real specific about it but why else would he never take up with no one in particular here?"

"Yes, it had somethin' to do with a woman, but I ain't gonna tell Stud's history to all and sundry. Sorry, Eva. I know you're a good woman, but Stud's kinda private about his past and wants to keep it that way. I need to be respectful of that. If he knows he's got your trust, he'll share on his own."

So much to process in one short conversation. My head was spinning through thoughts like a hamster on a wheel. I should have been feeling disgusted at the casual way Stud used women, but he did treat them with respect when he was with them. I knew some of them harbored feelings for the man, but I couldn't blame him entirely for that. The women he was with knew what they were getting into and did have the choice of saying no. While I thought Stud was an attractive man and would be thrilled to get his attention, I was not interested in joining the group of broken hearts he left in his wake, even if he was a gentleman about it. It made me wonder about what happened to make him that way.

A young boy with navy blue swim trunks and bright green plastic arm floaties ran up to our little group. He plonked his thin body next to Betsey and shivered.

"Water still a bit cold, punkin-head?" she asked, wrapping him in a towel.

He nodded, and she laughed, hugging him to her and rubbing his arms and chest briskly outside the towel.

"Let's get you warmed up! Prospect Sleeper is at the grill over yonder. Should have some burgers and dogs ready by now. You ready to get something to eat?"

The boy nodded vigorously, and Betsey laughed again, ruffling his wet hair into an even bigger mess that it already was.

"Eva, this here's my grandson, Cody. Cody? This is Eva. She's workin' on buildin' back the River's Edge Bar."

The boy suddenly burst out of the cotton cocoon his grandmother had rolled around him and ran to a tall, sandy-haired man wearing a deputy uniform who had entered the pool gate.

"Daddy!" he yelled and jumped at the man. Cody was caught easily and then settled on a lean hip, as if this maneuver had been done many times before. A little girl of maybe six or seven came running up, dripping wet, and plastered herself to his legs.

"Gotcha, buddy. Hey, sugar-drop." He placed a hand over the girl's head as she burrowed her face into his hip. He was oblivious to the water soaking into his uniform, just simply continued to hold his children close. I wasn't much into kids, but I still felt my heart twinge a bit at the love he openly showed.

A chorus of "Hey, Blue" went around the pool area.

This man was clearly the offspring of the club's matriarch and patriarch. He had inherited Betsey's height and Brick's solidity. I was betting Betsey's natural hair color was sandy blonde as the short buzzed hair on the top of Blue's head. His features were a blend of Betsey's beauty and Brick's roughness. Even in a plain khaki deputy's uniform, he looked hot.

"Hey, people," he replied in general.

"This is Eva. She's helping build the new River's Edge," Molly chimed in.

"Hey, Eva, nice to meet you," he distractedly greeted me. He reached out his free hand and shook mine briefly before turning his hazel eyes to Betsey.

"Mama, you gotta minute?"

Mama. He had to be a pretty secure man in order to call his mother "mama" at his age.

"No problem, baby." Betsey got up from her lounge and slipped on a pair of mules. *Jesus, Mary, and Joseph!* Did the woman ever wear anything below a four-inch heel? She threw a short red cover-up around her shoulders and followed Blue into the clubhouse, the mules slapping her feet.

"Jonelle is at it again," Molly informed Tambre and me. Since I didn't know who Jonelle was, I listened while Tambre sighed and shook her head.

"Bad news, that one," Molly continued. "Been married to Blue for nearly seven years and spent most of that draggin' him down. Been separated and back together more times than I got fingers. He finally got rid of her, and she's still making trouble for him."

"I'm sorry to hear that," I said, not really knowing what to do with this level of girl talk. It seemed a little more suited to the club's old ladies' inner-circle sisterhood than to be shared with a stranger. Thankfully Tambre interrupted.

"Church meeting is over. Boys are comin.'" She lifted her slim, lithe body out of the lounger and went to greet her old man.

A number of bikers were entering the pool area, some heading for the food-laden table and others toward the ladies around the water. Molly chirped at all of them, introducing me as if I were a celebrity.

Taz, Cutter, Bruiser, Table, Hollywood—the road names started blending with the faces and I was having a hard time keeping everyone straight. They all shook my hand but some of them lingered around the grinning Molly and me. Cutter kissed Molly and wandered off to the coolers and the food. Bruiser grunted a greeting and lumbered in the same direction. Table and Hollywood decided to stick around the pool for a bit. I recognized Table as the guy shooting pool the night I took out Nikki. He waved at me and pulled up a straight-back chair near where I was stretched out. I felt a little exposed.

"You work out a lot, huh?" Table asked, setting himself on the edge of his chair. He looked like a cue ball with his shaved head. The Fu Manchu was recently groomed and today he was wearing a charcoal gray sleeveless T-shirt under his cut, showing off his ink. I assumed he was referring to the size and definition of my arms.

"If you count slinging two-by-fours all day as working out, then yes." I sipped at my sweating tea.

He smiled a big white smile and I felt a flutter in my middle. He really was a good-looking guy.

"Name's Eva McAteer. Builder, finisher, and all-around grunt for Irish Pub Builders Inc."

"I'll be damned! Never met a woman who works construction. You do got some serious muscle definition." He didn't look like he was a stranger at the gym with his giant arms and shoulders. He settled back, only to be jostled when Hollywood dragged up another chair next to him. "I was thinking you did some boxing on account of the way you handled yourself with Nikki. Kinda curious now how much you'd bench press."

"You do gotta mean right hook," Hollywood declared, sitting

down as well. He pushed his Wayfarer sunglasses on top of his head, holding back his long dark hair like a headband. He looked a lot like a younger version of Johnny Depp's Captain Jack character... except with better teeth, which I guessed was why his road name was Hollywood. "I saw you lay out Nikki when she got in your face a few weeks back. She wasn't too happy 'bout it, but she had it coming for a long time."

I groaned a bit. "I didn't want to get into it with her. I really tried to get out of it, but once she took a swing at me...." I shrugged. "I don't particularly like to scrap but it's just not in my nature to back down from a fight."

A tall brute of a man wandered by, busily texting. He was handsome in his own way, but huge! Long dark hair pulled back in a ponytail, silver choker chain around his neck; he was frowning and glowering at everybody and everything.

"That's Mute." Table pointed his chin at the behemoth and grinned. "He don't talk much."

I remembered seeing him at the bar, filling the roll of club bouncer. "Looks like he's pissed at the world," I declared in a whisper. I had the feeling that getting Mute's attention was sometimes not a good thing.

"Nah, just worried 'bout his girl. She's pulling a double over at the hospital tonight, and he don't like it," Table said, still grinning. *Damn he has some white teeth!*

Betsey had mentioned Mute and Katrina to me before. Mute was her partner at the River's Edge bar. Katrina had started work there last summer and the two had been up and down for months before finally getting together. She also got caught up in the schemes of a former club member who was out to destroy the Dragon Runners. He had kidnapped her and gone on a wild ride through the famous Tail of the Dragon. Katrina had been badly injured in a wreck, common to those who didn't respect the Tail, and he had died in a fiery explosion.

I didn't say anything more. Just hummed and nodded along to let them know I heard. I wasn't exactly freaking out that two men were talking to me, but I didn't usually have men other than my brothers around me and more recently, Stud. I hadn't even had a hookup. I never felt comfortable about that kind of thing, and for years I really didn't have the opportunity even if I had the desire. Living in a tiny house separate from my brothers still didn't mean total privacy. I found myself enjoying the attention and I relaxed back into the lounge, sipping at the glass of melting ice cubes. I liked Stud—a lot—but I knew he wasn't really into me. How could he be with all those club women and practically every female he met falling at his feet?

"You shoot pool?" Table asked, leaning forward, placing his hands on his knees. "We got a table inside. I can teach you if you don't."

I smiled. *Challenge accepted!* "Let me break and you're on! Rack 'em up!" I jumped up from my prone position and bent over to retrieve my shorts and T-shirt. I heard one of the men next to me groan.

"Damn!" Hollywood muttered. "You have serious muscles all over. You sure you got them things just from working construction?"

Table was grinning from ear to ear. "I got a gym where I train couple times a week. You want, I can take you there and we can go a few rounds."

I looked him directly in the eye. *That's what she said* ran through my brain. What came out of my mouth was, "We *are* talking about boxing, aren't we?"

Table's grin got bigger. "Sure, baby girl. We're talking about boxing."

Baby girl?

"COWWWWWAAAAABUNNNH!"

The cry was accompanied by a large body hurling itself through the air and landing a cannonball in the pool right next to where I stood. The resulting splash barely reached the men but drenched me.

"Hear ye! Hear ye! Ladies of all ages! The dynamic duo, Patrick and Angus, are in the hoooouuuuse!" This announcement, made by Patrick, was followed by a second cannonball, nearly on top of Angus, and sent another huge wave of water over me.

"You fucking turds!" I yelled. My T-shirt was soaked through.

They just laughed and started splashing each other. The kids in the pool thought it was hilarious and started in as well, smacking the top of the pool surface, sending water everywhere.

"Pipe down, you hooligans!" Betsey called, clacking over in her high-heeled pool mules. "Leave the water where it is or else you ain't got nothin' to swim in later! Food's up, everyone! Grab it and growl!"

There was a small stampede as the kids and my two brothers scrambled out of the pool. Some ran dripping wet and some grabbed towels in their mad dash to be first in line at the food tables. I raised my hands up in the air as the small bodies hurtled around me and prayed my brothers wouldn't get the idea to toss me in. Apparently, God was busy.

"Last one, Eva! Rotten egg!" Angus crowed as both of them grabbed my waist and shoved me backwards.

"You fucking bast—" was as far as I got before the water closed over my head. I came up sputtering and furious. "Assholes!" I hoped Betsey didn't mind cursing around the kids. I'd heard it all my life, as my da hadn't held back an ounce.

"Jesus, you okay?" Table leaned over the pool and offered a hand. His face had lost its grin and he looked pissed. "I'll be your backup if you want to punch them out."

I heaved myself out of the pool and stood up, slopping water everywhere. "I'm good. I may take you up on your offer, though. Be nice to have some backup when I kick their sorry asses!"

"They always treat you this way?" Hollywood asked, his dark soulful eyes snapping in anger.

Really, these guys were cool.

"Yep, but I can take care of myself."

"Still ain't right," he muttered.

It was hard to believe these were bikers. I'd always heard MC men were rough and tough men who listened to and cared about no one but themselves and their club. Yet here I was with two Dragon Runners ready to throw down for me just because my dumbass brothers decided to toss me in a pool. I had to include Stud as well for being concerned about my back and shoulder, despite him having a woman with him when he came to see me. Then again, Stud always seemed to have a woman with him, while juggling another three.

Crap! Stop thinking about him, Eva!

I shrugged. "I'll dry quick enough."

"No need to wait, baby," Table said, bending over and slinging my pack over his massive shoulder. "We got a clothes dryer in the clubhouse. I'll loan you a T-shirt if you need it and you can hang in my room until your stuff dries. Come on and let me get you set up. I'll bring you a plate in a bit and we can eat there while your clothes dry."

He took my hand in his and smiled. He really was a nice guy. Hollywood looked like he would rather stick around, but he nodded at both of us before moving off toward the food tables.

I looked around as we headed toward the Lair and of course met the eyes of the last person I wanted to see when I was slinging water all over the place. Stud was stunned when he saw my condition and didn't bother to hide it. That changed when he spotted my pack over

Table's shoulder and his hand holding mine. His jaw got so tight I thought he would crack his teeth. I suddenly felt guilty, like I'd done something wrong.

He crossed his arms and sent Table a chilling look. "Just in case you didn't catch it earlier, she rode up here on the back of *my* bike."

Table grinned, but it wasn't a pleasant one. "That a fact? Well now, brother, that ain't much is it? You've had a lotta girls on the back of your bike. Never seen one stick."

Table stood nearly toe-to-toe with Stud, both men clearly not happy.

"Maybe this one will, maybe not. Not your call to make, *brother*." Stud spoke in a low growl that was worse than an angry yell. The menace in his voice was unmistakable. I'd never heard Stud get really mad. Irritated maybe, just a few times, but this was real anger and to tell the truth, it was kinda scary.

"She ain't claimed, brother," Table said, not backing down. "She ain't wearing a patch."

Oh my God! These two men were about to fight! A real one! Over—over me? Some women might get their egos stroked from that, but me? That's not just a no, that's a big, fat, *hell* no!

"Excuse me, people, but I don't speak biker! Patches, bikes, *claiming*? How 'bout I leave you two here and go find this clothes dryer myself while you guys enjoy your pissing contest?"

I went to slosh off into the clubhouse, but my dramatic exit was interrupted yet again. Betsey came running out of the clubhouse. "Stud! Nikki and that new girl Bambi are scrapping in there! Something about a sign-up sheet! What the hell have you done now?"

"Christ!" Stud muttered in both anger and disgust and shot me a look promising retribution before he stomped off toward the clubhouse.

I stifled a laugh behind my hand. Dramatic exit or not, that was perfect!

CHAPTER EIGHT

"**S**orry for getting in your business, Eva. Offer is still good for the dryer and the T-shirt. Start over?" Table asked, holding out his hand to me, palm up.

I looked at his face. He wasn't angry or pushy and the cold wet clothes were getting irritating. I smiled and took his meaty paw.

"Lead the way!"

Table led me into the large clubhouse. He did indeed have a room down a back hallway. There were eight of them on this side. He stopped at one that was midway down with his name on the front and opened the door.

"You leave it unlocked?" I asked.

Table chuckled and grinned at me. "I'm a full-patched Dragon Runner, baby. No one would steal from me, especially one of my own brothers. I trust every man here with my life."

The room looked like it was lived in; clean, but a little messy. Clothes were draped over the back of a chair and the footboard of the unmade bed. The floor was clear except for a set of dumbbells sitting in a far corner. A big poster of a vintage Harley motorcycle was taped to one wall and another of a large black panther was taped to another. I felt strange stepping over the threshold, like I'd just entered somewhere I really didn't belong.

"Here you go, baby." Table handed me a faded black Harley T-shirt and a pair of drawstring sweats. "These should do. You're almost as tall as me, but I bet my stuff will still swallow you."

I took the rolled-up pile. "Thanks, Table. I don't know what to say other than thank you."

He smiled and pointed at a closed door. "No problem. Bathroom is through there. How 'bout you grab a shower and I'll get us a couple plates. Food line is a bit long, so it will take me a while. Clothes dryer is in the closet at the end of the hall. Take your time."

I nodded. What else could I do?

I shook myself out and jumped in his shower, noting the high placement of the extra-wide head and multiple jet settings. Table enjoyed a few creature comforts. I used his soap and his 2-in-1 shampoo and conditioner, both having a masculine scent. There was only one towel hanging on the bar and I felt weird drying off with something I knew had been all over his body sometime earlier that day.

What the hell are you doing, Eva?

I didn't have to go commando as I did bring panties and a bra to change into with the intention of wearing the same shorts and T-shirt that were now sopping wet. Table wasn't back yet, and I didn't want to wait any longer than I needed to get underwear back on my ass. I wandered to the end of the hallway and found the washer and dryer in a closet with accordion folding doors. I dumped in my clothes, added a dryer sheet just because they were there, and started the timer.

A noise distracted me, and I glanced to my right. The door to the room next to me was cracked open and my heart dropped. It clenched in a pain that I didn't know was even possible. What's worse was that my head told me it didn't have a reason to be hurt, but that fucking organ apparently had a mind of its own.

I could see a sliver of Stud's profile as he stood in a bedroom almost identical to Table's. His shirt was off, and I could see the magnificent delineations of his pecs and abs. Unfortunately, I could also see a woman crouched in front of his open pants, eagerly sucking his cock. Stud's hand was wrapped around her bobbing head. I could hear the slurpy sounds she was making. Stud had his eyes closed, jaw and mouth tight. I recognized that frizzy blonde hair. It was Nikki!

I didn't know whether to cry or gag. This wasn't the first time I had seen a man get a blowjob. Wasn't even the first time I'd seen Stud get a blowjob. Living in close quarters with five men for so many years, there wasn't much I hadn't seen, heard, or smelled. While I lived in the RV, I could hear one or more of them masturbating and the amount of Kleenex they went through was astounding. After I moved out, they felt freer. I'd seen more than once, some woman Patrick or Angus had picked up at a bar sneaking from the RV in the early morning hours. I didn't have to imagine why they were there as they talked about it frequently. Owen had a collection of porn magazines I found once, and Garrett also had the occasional hookup but would go to the woman's place. I spotted him a few times coming back to the RV either very late in the night or very early before Da got up. Connor was even more discreet, and if he ever went with a woman, I didn't know about it as he didn't kiss and tell, and I hadn't caught him yet.

I punched the dryer button and the machine came to life loud and violently. I barely heard the surprised yelp from Nikki as I ran back down the hallway to Table's room. Yes, I was hiding, but at that point, I didn't care. I was hurt and telling myself I had no reason to be hurt. I knew Stud didn't want to be with just one woman. He was free and didn't have to answer to anyone about anything. He liked it that way and was happy. At least I assumed he was happy.

Fuck, Eva! Get it together and get over yourself!

I was sitting on the bed when Table knocked on the door.

"Eva? You find the dryer all right?" he asked, coming in with two plates balanced on his arm. The mouthwatering aroma of barbeque filled the air. I managed to put Stud out of my mind and smiled.

"Yup. Already started it. That smells fantastic!" I held the plates as Table pulled two beers from a mini fridge near his bed. I took a bite of the barbecue. Holy Mother of God! Sleeper, the prospect who was manning the grill, was pure genius! Sweet, tangy, smoky flavor burst in my mouth. I think I moaned.

We sat side by side on his bed, eating, drinking, and chatting. I found out Table worked as a tattoo artist and also did some boxing through a local gym.

"Some of my matches ain't exactly legal," he admitted with a wry smile, "but it's good money and I need all I can get right now. The wife and I split up last year and I'm trying to buy her out in the divorce. It ain't going too smooth, and she's being a real bitch 'bout everything. Helps that she lives down in Dilsboro. Haven't seen her in about eight months now. Just talking through lawyers at this point and biding my time until the divorce is final. Real pain in my ass." His eyes gazed into mine. "How you feel 'bout that?"

How did I feel about that? How was I supposed to feel about that?

"I'm sorry that's happening to you. It does sound like a lot of hassle," I said, and meant it. I was still unsure of where he was going with this line of conversation, but I had an idea.

He nodded and kept talking. "I'm being straight with you 'cause I'm interested. My life has a lot of baggage right now and any woman getting to know me needs to know that. I need you to tell me straight too, Eva, before I start talking again. You got somethin' going on with Stud?" he asked, his tone serious and his eyes boring deep.

I blinked and thought a moment about the kiss that Stud and I had shared just a few hours ago. It hadn't meant a thing to him, based on the goings-on in his room.

"Nope." I popped the *p*. "He's in the back getting a biker bunny blowjob right now from none other than Nikki the bottle-blonde bimbo. How's that for alliteration?"

Table choked. "Damn, baby! You don't pull back, do you?"

"I got five older brothers. What do you think?"

He chuckled and tipped his beer to his mouth, taking a swallow to clear his throat. "No, I guess you don't. Damn! Nikki? Christ almighty, that boy is messed up!" His face got serious. "I found out my wife cheated on me. More than once, so that's a deal breaker for me. I will not cheat, and I expect the same. I'll be honest in that I'm not ready to start something big with someone else 'cause technically I'm still married, but I'd really like to get to know you better."

I was both flattered and intimidated. My dating life had been nonexistent for so long, I wasn't sure how to handle this.

"I appreciate your honesty, Table." I looked him in the eye. "I'm not too sure of life myself right now, but I'm always down with making new friends. Start there?"

He smiled those gorgeous teeth at me. "Sounds good, baby. We still need to play that game of pool!"

We finished eating and he took the paper plates to dump in the main trash cans outside. I hesitated going back down the hall to get my clothes, but fuck it! I was a big girl and could handle anything. I still breathed a sigh of relief when I saw Stud's door hanging open to an empty room.

I went back to Table's room and started dressing. Ah! Nothing feels quite as good as putting on warm clothes fresh from the dryer!

I came out of Table's room smoothing my hands over my top and shorts and ran right into my father. Connor was right behind him, wearing a concerned look. I didn't realize what it looked like until Da screwed up his face in shock and anger.

"Jesus, Mary, and Joseph!" he yelled. "What are you doing alone in a man's room?"

If I wasn't so mortified, I would have rolled my eyes at his double standard. It was okay for his sons to fuck around, but anything involving me? He would be dragging me to a confessional for a deluge of "Hail Mary's" and "Our Father's," and we weren't even Catholic.

Not much was worse than having a parent embarrass you in front of people. What *was* worse was when one of those people was the man you wanted to avoid the rest of your life. Stud came around the corner and both saw and heard my da. His look was nothing short of furious, which made me angry as he, of all people, had no right to judge.

Connor looked at me with a weird expression. I'd said more than once to him during our brother-sister coffee chats that I was getting tired of being treated like I was still at a single-digit age. He was the only brother who seemed to acknowledge that I was a woman, but even he still had trouble recognizing I was no longer a child.

"You okay, Eva?" he asked, his face and mouth almost as tight as Da's.

How to deal with this? It never had been in me to back down from a fight.

"Of course I'm okay!" I exploded. "Table was helping me out while my clothes dried from being dunked by the asswipe twins! Anything else is no one's business!" I stomped down the hall and out of the door, with the intention of finding someone to drive me back down to my tiny house. *Grrr! Drama!*

***

Stud groaned and thrust deep into Nikki's hungry mouth as he came. She sucked in deep, swallowing every drop, then jumped back and squeaked when the dryer suddenly came to life, but neither of them saw who was in the hallway. She sat back on her knees and licked her puffy lips.

"You good, baby?" she purred.

He didn't know how to answer. He'd just come, sucked off by an expert, a woman he'd spent himself in many times, and yet felt nothing. Not a shred of satisfaction. Why was he even doing it? Couldn't be because he spotted Eva holding hands with Table. Jealously was not in his nature. She didn't belong to him. He was a free agent and could fuck whomever he wanted, right?

"Yeah, sweetheart, I'm good," he said automatically. Nikki didn't notice his lack of conviction.

"Knew you'd come back to me. Ain't no woman better'n me for you," she huffed as she stood and started stripping. "Ain't no Bambi hussy gonna take my man."

Stud stared at her. Overbleached hair, thick makeup trying to cover her bad skin tone and deepening wrinkles, and a body that was way too skinny. Ribs and protruding hip bones had him thinking she needed to lay off the booze and the drugs. She looked like a street hustler trying to find her next fix.

"Ain't no dyke gonna take my man either!" she declared as she climbed on his bed and flopped on her back. She drew her knees up and spread her legs wide, presenting him with a full view of her bare pussy. She fingered herself, stroking between her legs and moaning dramatically, giving him a real show.

"This is all for you, baby. My man, Stud," she crooned as her fingers moved. "My old man, Stud."

He should have been turned on. He should have been ready to go again. He should live up to his name and jumped on the writhing woman spreading herself for his pleasure.

Instead he felt numb. Empty.

"Time to go, Nikki," he announced in a dead voice while he tucked himself away and zipped up his jeans.

Her hands stopped moving between her legs and she blinked up at him owlishly. "What?"

"You're not coming in my room or my bed anymore. I'm done."

"You're teasin' me, aren'tcha, baby?" she whined, pushing out her lower lip in what was supposed to be a sexy pout. It didn't work.

"I'm serious. This is it. I'm not your old man and never will be. You might even want to take a break from the club. Get yourself clean. Whatever you're on isn't doing you any good," he said as he picked up her clothes and tossed them on the bed next to her.

He tuned out the rest of what she was saying while she cussed and dressed. Thoughts swirled in his brain, looping over themselves and twisting like snakes. Eva and Table. He was a good man who was dealing with a lot of shit right now. Maybe Eva could handle it, maybe not. He was more suited than Stud to be an old man, better at committing, better man all the way around. Eva was a good woman and didn't realize her own potential. Any red-blooded man would see her worth and want that for himself. Why didn't he want it for himself? He had baggage too. More than Table? *Yes. Maybe.*

Don't know. All those nights talking, watching movies and Netflix series, the comfortable space he shared with Eva… was there more? He found Eva fascinating and the more time he spent with her, the more time he wanted to spend with her. Did he even deserve it?

Nikki finished dressing and huffed her way to the door.

"You'll come back to me again, baby. You always do." She smirked and left.

Stud felt nothing.

He paused a moment and walked out into the hallway, his thoughts still whirling as he spotted Table carrying two full plates of barbecue. He shuffled the plates, balancing them on his arm so he could knock on his own door. Stud felt a two-by-four hit him in the solar plexus when Eva opened the room and smiled at Table. She was wearing his clothes! She took a plate from him and backed into the room. Table followed, closing the door behind him.

Stud's jaw got so tight his teeth were ready to crack. Nope. Didn't matter to him what Eva was doing in Table's room. Not a bit. He tamped down the urge to burst through the closed door and beat the ever-lovin' shit out of his club brother and stalked outside to his bike. He had the urge to fire it up, drive up to the Tail, and take a hard ride, but he managed to quell it. The Tail of the Dragon was a fierce mistress who demanded respect. Riding on her angry and reckless could cost you dearly, even your life. He'd already experienced what the Tail would do to anyone riding her without complete focus. He'd been flirting with a woman he was carrying on the back of his bike when a deer ran out in front of them and he'd had a nasty wreck. She had been okay, but he had paid with a broken arm and twisted ankle. That was mild in comparison to what it could have been.

Stud breathed in deeply as he ran his hands over the sleek lines of his bike, forcing himself to calm down and think. Eva and Table. Yes, they were a good fit. Eva and Stud. Not such a good fit. Simple as that. Yet he was drawn to her, and the thought of letting her go to be with his brother twisted his gut in a knot.

He stood there a while, just stroking his bike and listening to the distant sound of the kids who were back in the pool. He realized he left his helmet in his room and would need it if he decided to go for ride in any capacity. He went back in the Lair and heard Fergus's bellow. Coming down the hallway, he spotted the man, Connor and a red-faced Eva. It was clear she was being dressed down by her father, and it was equally clear, she was not having any of it. The look on her face when she spotted him sent a ball of dread dropping through his body to his toes. She saw him with Nikki. *Fuck!*

"Of course I'm okay! Table was helping me out while my clothes dried from being dunked by the asswipe twins! Anything else is no one's business!" Stud felt her words hit him like bullets. She stomped down the hall and left all three men standing there. Fergus blustered something, but Stud didn't really pay attention to it. Connor looked ready to chase after her but held himself back. He glanced at Stud, his manner one of frustration. Both MacAteer men finally left, and Stud really didn't care where they went.

"Hey, Stuuuudd!"

He turned to see Bambi coming down the back hall and waving at him. Stud looked at her fiercely for a moment and mentally tallied the remaining condom supply in his room. Best way to get over a woman was to get in another, right? He learned that lesson a long time ago.

Then why did he feel like shit?

He made a decision that would surprise anyone in the club who knew him. It even surprised him. He smiled gently and shook his head at the hopeful look in Bambi's eyes. Instead of losing himself between the thighs of a random woman, he went to his room and got his helmet. A hard run on the Tail sounded better than risking the heart of the young girl any further. Maybe it was time to rethink his habits.

CHAPTER NINE

Fuck my life! **I thought** viciously as my foot slipped a bit again. Garrett and Owen were putting in the wood flooring, Connor and Da were checking the wiring as Da was the electrician of our crew, and I was on the roof of the new River's Edge Bar, setting cement around the stones that framed the chimney. Even though it was stone veneer, we still needed to make it as authentic-looking as possible. I unfortunately got put on the building team with Patrick and Angus, and of course drew the short straw to go up on the roof. This did not fill me with joy—I was sick of the drama that seemed to want to follow me.

It was Friday morning, only five short days after the barbecue at the Lair. It was amazing how much had happened in just five days.

On Monday, Table had come to the job site, rumbling up on his black and silver Harley.

"Hey, Eva, what's shakin'?" he had asked, pulling off the small helmet some called a brain bucket. There wasn't a lot of it there and I wondered how much protection it would provide in a real crash.

"This damn miter saw, that's what! Blade's been running rough all day, but the boss doesn't want to put money into a new one." I shot a pointed look at Da, who was standing by one of the finished walls. Connor was with him, ticking off measurements and running a plumb line to check for straightness.

"How are you?" I asked.

"I'm good." He grinned and then winced as I drew the circular blade down, forcing it to bite into the two-by-four at an angle. The saw screamed in protest and I had to grip the piece harder in my work glove to make it stay put. "Damn, baby! Sounds like you're killing it!"

"Nope, we're just fighting a bit. But I'm going to win," I grunted as the piece finally cut, not as cleanly as I would have liked, but until Da coughed up a new blade I had to make do.

"Ha! Told you!" I crowed, holding the angled cut up like it was show-and-tell.

He grinned at me. "No doubt. Speaking of winning, we never did get that pool game in yesterday. You busy tonight? We can go grab a bite at this Mexican place I know over in Maggie Valley and play a few games at the bar."

"Is this like a real date?" I asked, tossing the piece and picking up another one.

He preened. "It's not like a real date, it *is* a real date. Dinner and a game of pool instead of dinner and a movie."

Something about using the D-word felt really, *really* wrong.

Maybe it was because Stud appeared in the work trailer's doorway. He took off his nerd glasses and stared hard at Table. I guessed we were done. No more surprise visits with food or beer, no throwing microwave popcorn at each other while arguing the intricacies of sci-fi films, no cuddles, and no more kisses.

Stud had been really short with me the couple of times I had to speak to him this morning. He could just be having a bad day, but it was such a change from how he normally treated me that I had to wonder. It couldn't have been anything to do with that confrontation he had with Table at the party, could it? What was that even about—I still didn't speak biker, but if it was about me, and that's why Stud was being a dick this morning, he needed to get over himself. He'd been with more than one woman since I'd met him. Fuck that!

"I—um—no, I don't have plans. I'll go on a date with you."

I went out with Table that Monday night to a Mexican place about a half hour's ride on the back of his big black Harley—which was a blast! I was so getting a bike of my own as soon as I could. Table was the perfect gentleman. Even with his scary biker look, which seemed to intimidate everyone at the restaurant, he was polite and nice. He opened doors for me, guided me through the maze of tables with a hand at my waist, let me order first, held my hand any chance he got, and when we went to a local bar to shoot pool, he let me break the first game. We talked, smiled, and laughed. He was a terrific man, and I felt comfortable enough with him to share my secret love of sewing. I really was starting to like him.

The date was great and ended with a long, wet kiss in front of my tiny house. That was it. No pushing to spend the night or take it to the next level. He came to my place Tuesday night and we watched a movie curled up on my sofa bed. It felt strange to be curled up next to Table instead of Stud, but it was obvious to me that he was done. I couldn't say it didn't hurt, but I also knew it wasn't my problem.

Table talked about his soon-to-be ex-wife and his shitty marriage. I talked about my life on the road. He told me his real name was James. I showed him the quilt I had started, and he seemed impressed.

"I have a queen size at my place, babe. No particular color scheme," he said, his eyes sparkling. "Just saying."

When he kissed me, he did it soft and stealthily. His lips molded to mine, and he flicked his tongue against them until I opened for him. I could feel the excitement build in both of us. I squirmed against him, wanting more, and found myself on my back with him pressing me into the cushions. My mouth was full of his taste and my body on fire. One of his hands drifted upwards and covered my breast, flicking my nipple back and forth with his thumb. I gasped into his mouth at the electricity shooting through me. He pulled down the shoulder of my tank top, and my bra strap with it. He sucked my nipple into his mouth while rolling the other between his fingers and I cried out at the sensations that set the nub of flesh between my legs pulsing with unfamiliar need. I was ready to panic, but didn't want this ache to stop.

He let go of my nipple with a soft pop. Breathing hard, he closed his eyes as if pulling himself back into control.

"Separation papers are filed, but technically I'm still married, sweetheart," he said, threading his fingers through my mine and looking directly in my eyes. "You know I gotta thing about cheaters. I want you bad, but I can't until I'm fully divorced. It's happening real soon. Can you wait?"

Yeah, I can wait. I also can't wait!

It went to shit Thursday night.

It started out okay. Table picked me up in his truck after a long workday, and we went into town for dinner and to the temporary bar for drinks and pool. Stud's band was playing, and he was fiddling on stage with his equipment when we arrived. He had his normal bunch of groupies around him vying for attention, but he still noticed when Table and I walked in. He frowned when Table put his arm around me and pulled me close, staking a public claim. Stud didn't speak to me or even look in my direction. Fuck him!

I wasn't sure about a future between Table and me, but I was starting to hope there was one. I was really beginning to like him. He was a good man, one with a lot of integrity, which was a rare thing. Being coupled with him wouldn't be bad, as I knew he would always treat me well.

A short blonde woman walked in while I was lining up a tricky shot. She was dressed in old jeans and a faded Harley T-shirt. Normally she wouldn't stand out in a biker bar, except she had a diaper bag over one arm and one of those baby carrier thingies on the other. Not too many parents would bring babies to a bar. She scanned the room, and when her eyes landed on Table and me, her mouth turned down and she strode over to us with purpose. I felt a cold lump settle in my gut. Something was about to happen that may not be so good.

"Table!" she shouted, getting his and everyone else's attention.

She gave me a hard look and pointedly raised her nose. *Really?*

"What the fuck do you want?" Table growled, not bothering to look at her. He was eyeing the baby carrier. This was the soon-to-be-ex. He stood next to the pool table, clutching his cue stick between furious white knuckles. Table hadn't hidden anything from me, and I trusted him. Somehow I knew the baby was a surprise to him.

"We need to talk!" she shouted again, lugging the carrier and the bag to where we were playing.

"I don't gotta do nothin' for you," he snapped back, moving around the table and looking at the pattern of balls. It was clearly a gesture of dismissal, but I noticed his hands were shaking.

"Yeah, you do. Turns out, the kid is yours." She jostled the carrier containing the now squirming bundle. The baby made a few noises and rubbed a tiny hand over its face.

Table finally looked at her, stunned. "What?"

"It ain't Jack's or Mark's or Richie's. Only one left is you. DNA test is quick over at t' hospital, iffen you want to make sure, but you're the only one left. Gotta be yours."

She set the carrier and the bag on the pool table, jostling several balls out of place. Neither I nor Table said anything.

"Tim's outside. We're heading to the coast. Papers are in the bag for custody. Divorce ones is still on the way only 'cause they make you wait a whole year. All you gotta do is sign 'em and mail 'em. I'm outta here."

She turned and started walking away.

"Wait a minute!" Table exploded. "You're just going to walk out and leave—leave—fuckin' shit! What's the kid's name?"

"It's a girl. I call her Angie. You can change it if you want. I don't care. Put your last name on the birth certificate already. I gotta go. Tim's waitin' for me."

"You're just going to leave her here? With me?" Table looked like a ton of bricks just landed on his head. "What the fuck are you doing? You can't just go run off and leave your baby!"

The woman rolled her eyes, cocked out a hip, and rested a taloned hand on it. "Sure I can. I never wanted to be no mama, and Tim sure as hell don't wanna be no daddy. You were always talking about family and lotsa kids. Now's your chance. Good luck!"

She walked out of the bar without a second thought or even a glance at the baby she was leaving behind.

He set the cue stick down and moved to take the tiny bundle in his large hands. I could feel my heart breaking a bit. I didn't think I'd fallen in love with Table, but I also had grown close to him and was warming up to the idea of us being a real couple. Something I'd never had. Those giant working hands cradled the soft pink bundle with such care, I knew he was lost. His eyes rose to mine.

"Eva." His look and voice were strained. That would be expected when your world suddenly shifted gears from first to tenth.

"I'll call Betsey. She'll know what to do," I said, pulling out my phone.

Betsey said she was on her way. I watched Table cradle the tiny pink bundle. His club brothers came by to look and the band was silent as the drama continued. I felt Stud's presence as he came and stood by Table. His eyes looked strange and glossy as he stared at the baby. She fussed a bit and screwed up her face as if gearing up to cry.

Table gave her a finger to grip and she immediately tried to put it in her mouth. Stud rummaged through the bag and found a bottle of formula ready to go and a few diapers. How thoughtful of the raging bitch that was this poor kid's mother.

Table plugged the bottle into the baby's mouth and she quieted immediately.

"Eva. This changes things," he said quietly. "I really like you. I like you a whole lot, but I've got a whole new circumstance that I do not know how to handle just yet. I can't bring someone new in my life when I just found out I have a daughter. Tamara never told me she was pregnant, but I don't need a DNA test to prove anything. I know she's mine. I hope you'll forgive me."

I smiled at him. My heart wasn't exactly breaking, but it still hurt. I did understand where he was coming from, and I admired him for stepping up and doing what was right.

"Nothing to forgive. She's cute. Got your head of hair," I joked, touching the light fuzz covering the baby's bald head.

He smiled and chuckled as Betsey arrived. I didn't know what the club brothers would do without her. She came in and took charge, taking over the baby like it was one of her own grandchildren. Table wanted the baby to ride in his truck back to the Lair but didn't want to leave me stranded.

"I got her," Stud stated solemnly. "Band doesn't need to play and Mute's thinking about closing early. Doesn't seem the best of occasions to party. I'm really sorry you're dealing with that bitch, but congratulations on being a dad. It's a helluva thing, brother."

He clapped a hand on Table's meaty shoulder.

The car seat was firmly secured onto the bench seat I'd occupied a few hours ago. Strains of the Queen song "Another One Bites the Dust" ran through my head as Table hugged me.

"Still friends?" he asked.

What else can I do?

"Always." I smiled, willing myself to look relaxed and okay with life.

He climbed into the cab and took off. Betsey followed.

Me? I proceeded to get rip-roaring drunk. I didn't do that often. Working at the job site through a hangover is both miserable and dangerous, but at that moment, I really didn't care. I had to wrap myself around Stud like a second skin to keep from falling off as I rode with him on the back of his bike. So what if I ran my hands all over his stomach and chest? It was a safety situation!

I was singing "Danny Boy" as I threw my leg over the bike, "*Oh Dannneeeboyeeee, da pipes da pipez'er caw-awling!*" and nearly pitched headfirst into the parking lot gravel. "Oopz! Sorry 'bout th' song. Thas all I know."

Yes, I even giggled.

Stud wasn't having it. His face stayed aloof and unsmiling as he got off, kicking out the stand to lean the bike over. He was still sober. *Party pooper!*

"You gonna be all right? I've never seen you like this since you've been here."

I screwed up my face and flipped my hand. "Nah! Am good. Doncha know by now? Am Eva MacAteer! Am every wonz frien!"

I threw out my arms in what was supposed to be a grandiose move and almost ended up on my ass again. Stud caught me and dragged me upward.

"Let's get you in bed before you fall down." He took my key, unlocked my house, and pushed me inside. "You gonna barf?"

"Maybe." I burped. My lady lessons were sadly lacking. "Doan matter, Ah'll geddup inna mornin' and report for duty as always. Hee-hee-hee! Ah said doody!"

Stud almost smiled at my slurred joke that was more suited for a first grader. I was happy to see it. Happy enough to share my wise thoughts with him as any drunk woman would.

"Aryoo still mad at me?" I flopped on my couch and slid to my side. Staying upright was just too much. "Ah doan wan yoo ta be mad at me. Ah doan like it when yer mad. Ah liked it bedder when we were frins."

"I'm not mad, Eva," he said, pulling a quilt over me. The same one we both had draped over ourselves when we were movie buddies.

I burped again. "You really needta stop treatin' women like that," I informed him sagely. I was sure the burping ruined the effect, but

ML NYSTROM

at the time everything made perfect sense. "And y'also need da stop lettin'em treat you that way too."

Stud blinked and stiffened. "You're not drunk enough to tell me what to do, Eva."

I kept on. "You doan ged it! You luuuuuv women, and treat them sooooo nice when ur with 'em. But winna woman starts ta think mebbe she'z special to you, poof! She'z gone an' yoo fin' anudder one. Itz like a colleshun, collec-shun, a collackt-shum. You ged da word! You can't handle jus' one! Mebbe one ada time! Hee-hee-hee!"

Stud wasn't amused at me this time.

"I can't blame yoo mush. Da women yur with make you inno a trophy, too! Zere jus' as bad! Always chasin' yoo like you're sum sorta trophy. Itza big deal at the club to bang the Stud! Hey! Tha' kinda rhymes!"

Why is it I was so much smarter when I was drunk? I grabbed at Stud's hand because he really needed to pay attention and hear my smartness. "Yur a speshul man, an' shud be treated rite."

I was losing it. The alcohol was in full swing, hitting me hard.

"Ah wish Ah was speshul," I intoned, forgetting for a moment I had an audience and I was talking out loud. I was fading fast. I'd never been a wild drunk and very seldom got this bad. Time for me to pass out before I shared more wisdom than I should.

The world tilted on its axis and I went out like a light. The last thing I heard—or thought I heard—was Stud saying, "You are more special than you think, Eva."

Fast forward to this morning.

Patrick and Angus, of course, hearing over the grapevine I had a rough night and was hungover like hell, made it their mission to annoy the bejezus out of me by flicking the pulley rope at me or throwing me tools that were just barely within reach.

"Quit fucking around, you two jackasses!" I yelled at them irritably as Patrick flicked the rope just as my hand touched it to pull out another stone from the swinging bucket. The best way we had to haul the heavy rocks to the roof was to rig a pulley system to the chimney framework and pull a heavy bucket up from the ground. Patrick was in charge of putting the stones in the bucket and getting them to me. Angus was mixing the cement that also made its way to me. Eventually, one of them was supposed to come up to the roof, bring me a new safety harness, and add his hands to the work. The one I had on had a bad frayed spot I didn't notice earlier when I was strapping in. So far today, both of them had come up with excuse after excuse for why they couldn't be the ones to climb the ladder and join me. They never did bring me that new harness.

"Eva, lass, you're doin' such a fine job, I'd hate to go up there and mess it up!" Angus laughed. "Here's another trowel for you. You can have one in each hand!" He tossed up a wide flat cement smoother and I had to duck so it wouldn't hit me.

"Asshole!" I yelled at him angrily. The slick cement was mixed with too much water so it was running off and the stones were slipping out of place. Not to mention I was covered with the stuff, as I'd managed—with a little help from them—to get splattered head to toe. "Make this shit right, Angus! I'm not in the mood to play, you fuckwad! Let's just please get this done!"

"Ooh! Eva got a hot date tonight? Maybe Angus is getting you back for cockblocking him at the club last time we were there!" Patrick yelled up, laughing. This earned him a wad of cement in the face from Angus.

"Hey, dumbass! I got in there, all right? She couldn't keep her hands or her mouth off me!" he preened.

"What was her name again?" Patrick garbled around the cement he was spitting out.

"How the hell should I know?" Angus laughed.

"I'm in the fucking twilight zone!" I muttered, slapping a sinking stone back in place. I was about to yell at them again when a familiar sound hit my ears. The roar of Stud's Harley announced his arrival to the job site. I swallowed any further comments and troweled more cement around the chimney, trying not to look in his direction. Fuck my life! I did not know how to handle this, knowing he'd seen me at a really low point, drunk off my ass and saying crap I had no business saying. Men and women. Dating. Feelings. Kissing. Not kissing. *Gah! Drama!*

I risked a glance in his direction and caught him frowning at me up on the roof. I couldn't see it, but I imagined his lips tightening in disapproval. He moved into the building, I was supposed to meet with Connor and Da. I stared for a moment and then, stiffening my jaw, kept working. Who was he to judge me?

"Eva, your stones are slipping out!" I heard a split second before one of the stones in the milky cement fell out and hit my head and shoulder. That might not have been so bad, but the strike threw me off balance and tumbled me off the roof. The safety harness held for a moment and then snapped. I didn't even have time to curse. I fell fifteen feet and landed flat on my back and shoulders. My head bounced off the pavement, and I didn't just see stars, I saw fucking galaxies. I heard loud raucous laughter coming from Patrick and Angus through the ringing in my ears, but couldn't move. I could only lay there, one big bundle of shock, as in slow motion, the stones I had painstakingly tried to keep in place slid off the wet chimney. I had a split second to think *oh shit, this is gonna hurt* before a dozen or so heavy stones fell on me. I felt something give in my ribcage and something else bury itself in my left leg. *Fuckers!* I thought, fighting to get breath enough to scream at them that I was really hurt. I couldn't breathe. *Come on, Eva. Breathe.* Nothing. No voice. No breath. Fuck me, I'm going to die right here on a job site with my asswipe brothers laughing at me for falling off a roof.

I heard a roar. Actually, maybe two roars. I wasn't sure. I did know the pressure around my ribs finally lightened and I was able to

draw in a breath. Then the real pain hit. *Fuck me! Fuck me! Fuck ME!*
Someone knock my ass out! I fought it, trying to get up, trying to run
from it. I gagged with it, which didn't help my ribs any. *Holy fucking*
shit, someone please *knock my ass out!*

"Be still, baby, be still." Stud was holding me down, cradling my
face in his hands while Connor lifted and threw away the stones that
covered me. "I know it hurts bad, but you have to stay awake."

"I don't want to!" I managed to wheeze. "If you're any kind of
fucking friend, punch my lights out!"

"That's my girl. Keep arguing with me, Cactus. Ambulance is on
the way." His mouth grimaced in an attempted smile, but it didn't
reach his eyes. There was fury and fear in them.

"Ah, Christ, look at her leg!" Connor said, putting pressure on
it. White-hot agony zapped a sudden lightning strike in my lower
half and I screamed.

"Fuck! Fucking hell!"

"Don't touch it! It may be the only thing plugging the main
artery. Keep her still, Stud, and I'll get a tourniquet going." Someone
knelt beside me and started wrapping something. I was drifting a
bit, then whatever they did nearly brought me straight up.

"Son of a motherfuckin' bitch!" I yelled, my ribs protesting the
sudden movement. My head spun, and my vision was going gray.

"Wait, what? Is she really hurt?" Angus asked in a bewildered
little boy voice.

"What do you think, you stupid fuck?" Stud growled at him, still holding me. "Baby, stay awake. Argue with me, fight with me, get mad as hell at me, but please stay awake."

I was floating between consciousness and unconsciousness. Passing out seemed like a good idea, even though Stud didn't want me to do it. Maybe I was going to die. I looked at his eyes, the only thing left I had that I could focus on.

"I really miss you." My tongue was thick, and I was having trouble making the words come out. I didn't even know if I sounded coherent. I stopped fighting the creeping blackness and let myself slide into it.

CHAPTER TEN

Stud paced in the hospital waiting room, trying to contain his anger. He was there along with Betsey and Tambre. One phone call and the club women always rallied to take care of everyone. Stud had followed the ambulance on his bike from the half-finished bar. Eva's father had insisted her brothers stay and keep working on the site.

"No sense in all of us going. Too much time lost, and we're a man down now," he stated as he motioned his sons to get back to work.

Connor lost it before Stud could.

"Are you out of your mind?" he yelled, throwing his arm out and pointing to Eva's broken form. "Your daughter is lying there injured, and you're worried about a fucking job!"

"We have to be in Wilmington for another one in three weeks! We can't afford any down time!" the old man yelled back.

Connor blinked in surprise. "What the hell are you talking about? We're nowhere near being finished here! Is that why you've been pushing us to spend every waking minute on the site? Because you fucked up and cross-booked another job?"

Fergus threw his hands wide in a dismissive gesture. "I didn't look at the calendar. The Wilmington job is a big one. Four resort hotel bar remodels, one after another." He huffed. "We can still get this one done if we keep up our pace. Eva's already got the bar construction done on the inside. Owen and Garrett can do the rest of the finish work, while the rest of you shingle the roof. I've almost finished the wiring in the interior walls."

"Un-fucking-believable!" Connor threw his hands in the air, the movement similar to his father's as the old man walked away. He stood for a moment, anger radiating off him in waves. If the look he shot his father's retreating back could burn, the older man would have been incinerated on the spot.

"God fucking dammit! I hate this shit! I'm so goddamned tired of it!" Connor turned to Stud who was still crouched over Eva's still form. Pain ravaged his face, making him look much older than his thirty-four years. In one of their nighttime conversations, Eva had talked to Stud about Connor being the glue that was holding the family together. The brothers were depending on him to keep the company going for their livelihood as their father was getting older and starting to make mistakes. This was a heavy burden to carry, and Stud could see the man buckling under the weight of it. Stud got the impression Connor wanted nothing more than to tell Fergus to go to hell and go to the hospital with Eva, but there was still a job site that had to be shut down properly and no one else but him to see that it got done.

"Would you please make sure the hospital does right by her and call me? Not him?" Connor's voice ground out like he had a mouthful of gravel. "I'll get this shit straightened out here and get there as quick as I can."

Stud didn't say anything to the struggling man. He just gave a short nod.

The ambulance showed up and the paramedics took charge. Stud had hoped Kat would be working the emergency room. She was one of the most competent people he knew, and he could trust her.

Stud turned and paced in the other direction, his mind both racing and numb at the same time.

"Miss Eva MacAteer?"

Betsey stood up when the doctor entered the small waiting room and Stud stopped his pacing to focus on the man.

"Not as bad as it should have been. X-rays show two cracked ribs, which is remarkable given the fall and the weight of the stones.

Lots of bruises, so she'll be sore and breathing will be hard, but I don't see any major internal damage. I was expecting full breaks and a lot of them."

Betsey clapped her hands. "Lord have mercy! That's good news!"

Stud was both relieved and irritated. It sounded like the doctor was disappointed there wasn't more injury. "Yeah. She'll try harder next time," he said drily.

The doctor cleared his throat and continued.

"She is concussed, but her pupils are normal and her responses are good. She has a severe laceration on her left thigh, but not as deep as we originally thought. The stone did not pierce the main artery. A few other smaller cuts and scrapes, but nothing serious. She's being stitched up and will need to stay overnight for observation, but I'm relatively sure she can go home tomorrow."

Home. Stud thought about it and turned to Betsey.

"Give her my room at the Lair. Only makes sense. Her house is not set up for this, her family obviously can't take care of her, and you've got too much happening between the club, the bar, Brick, and Blue's shit with Jonelle. Plus, you're still working on Kat and Mute's wedding."

"All that's true, darling." Betsey blinked. "And I was thinking the same thing about the Lair, but lettin' her use Table's room since he left for Asheville this morning. He decided to go back to his grandma's place for a bit for some help with the baby and to get his head together. He won't be back for a while and that leaves us a space to use."

"No," Stud said firmly. The thought of Eva in Table's room and ultimately in Table's bed, even if she was alone in it, was completely repugnant to him. It was not going to happen.

"But if you ain't got a room, where you gonna sleep? And who's gonna take care of Eva when I cain't?"

Stud loved that about Betsey. Always ready to help someone, club or not.

"I still have a condo out in the big development, the one I rent out all the time to tourists, but this week it's free and I can take it off the rental site for a while. I'll make the commute if I need to, or stay in whatever guest cabin in the compound is open. Eva will be better off in the main lodge with more people around. As far as taking care of her, I plan on doing a lot of it."

Betsey pursed her lips, lowered her chin, and looked at Stud with both eyebrows raised. Brick called it her mama bear face. She crossed her arms in front of her body and spoke in a low don't-mess-with-me-I'm-serious voice. "You're a growed-up man and a good one, Stud, but I do got eyes in my head. I ain't seen you like this over a woman before, and I'm sure as the day is long, if it were Nikki or that new girl Bambi in there, you wouldn't be out here walking up and down like a bad-tempered bull. I reckon you got some feelings for this girl, and if that is true, then I'm happy for you, but I'm gonna have my say in that this ain't no episode of Stud's angels where you need a blonde, brunette, and redhead chasing after you. I've spent enough time with her to know Eva ain't no woman who's gonna chase any man. Table was right interested and would've been good for her, but that's out now. If you're gonna step in, by all means, but you just make sure this ain't no pissin' contest 'cause Table stepped in first."

Stud met Betsey's look head on. Her words made him furious. This was his business, and she had no right telling him how to handle it. But this was Betsey and he knew that when it came down to brass tacks, she had his back. The club was still tight no matter what.

"Nikki is out. She needs to be gone for good from the Lair. Last few times I've seen her she's been more than drunk. She's been tweaking on something, and anyone in this club knows that's not done here out of respect for you and your house."

Betsey relaxed her posture and face.

Stud kept his eyes steady on hers. "Bambi is of legal age but still way too young to be around us. She's more fascinated with the club than with me. Been with more than just me as well. She thinks life's a constant party and if she's not careful, she'll end up like Nikki. She's still a good kid and could use some mama love."

Betsey nodded, taking the hint.

Stud kept his voice even, but there was a core of steel in his tone. "As far as Eva is concerned, that's my business and no one else's."

CHAPTER ELEVEN

I clicked the remote, changing channels rapidly on the ginormous Lair television. Daytime talk shows, news feeds, soap operas, even cartoons flashed by, but nothing held my interest. I couldn't work the site for obvious reasons, I couldn't walk too far as my ribs and leg would protest loudly, I couldn't swim in the pool because of the stitches, I couldn't sleep because for the entirety of my life, I'd gotten up at the butt crack of dawn for work or school or both. Bleh! It was only one week after my fall and for the first time ever, I was bored. Not just bored. *Bored!*

I huffed and tossed the remote to the side. Sesame Street was the show the TV had landed on and a couple of colorful puppets were singing about being friends. All I heard was blah, blah, blah. I rested my head on the back of the couch and closed my eyes, tuning out the high-pitched voices of the children's show.

My da and Connor had come by the hospital when I was getting out and brought me to the Lair. Patrick and Angus had visited me as well, bringing me a butt ton of flowers, and telling me how sorry they were. This was the most contrite I'd ever seen them. Garrett and Owen told me when they came by that Connor had reamed Patrick and Angus's asses hard enough, they probably would be feeling it for months. I didn't care at first and was angry as hell at them, but they seemed to be genuine in their remorse about what happened. Patrick and Angus not giving me shit was completely foreign to me. They didn't even try to joke with me about laying out of work because of the injury, which made me wonder if they were feeling all right.

I spent two days in the hospital before getting sent "home" to the Lair. I wanted to protest loud and long, but knowing Connor's position and Da's stubbornness, I didn't have a chance. Not to mention Betsey insisted I stay there while I was healing. I was put in Stud's room and tried to protest loud and long again but was overruled. I thought Table's room was open, but Stud informed me rather firmly that it had been reserved by another club member.

It bothered me more to be in his room because I knew what he did in the bed that I was now occupying. Could I say why? Probably not. Stud's activities weren't my problem. I wasn't involved and didn't want to be involved. But still, picturing him in the room, naked in all his mouthwatering glory, touching, tasting, kissing and— Gah! Fuck my life!

"Tired or bored?" I heard a soft voice say. "Since it's before nine, I'm guessing bored."

I lifted my head and opened one eye. Kat, the club's unofficial nurse and soon-to-be bride of Mute, the official club bouncer and chief badass, had arrived along with Molly. These women were definitely the elite among the club women, and I liked them a lot.

Kat motioned for me to stand up and slip down my super loose lounge pants. These were ones I made that had little cartoon ducks on them. What can I say? The fabric was on clearance at the time. I grimaced at the painful pull in my leg before I sat back down. I was sure I presented a lovely picture, sitting on the couch in a fluffy white robe with duck pants around my ankles. Thank God no one else was around. If Patrick were here, I'd already be posted on Facebook as a meme!

She changed the dressing and smeared some white goop over the stitches to keep them from itching so bad.

"The wound looks really good. I can't believe how fast you're healing!" she remarked, taping another gauzy square over the crusty, gooey mess.

"That looks good? You're out of your mind!" I laughed, then

winced as my ribs caught me. "Shit! Not fast enough though! Damn, I hate being like this!"

"I don't blame you, sugar," Molly sympathized. "This one time when Cutter was younger, he laid down his bike and messed up his leg. Bad, and I do mean bad! Broke the big bone and cracked the two little ones. He's got enough pins in him to set off airport alarms."

"Femur, tibia, and fibula," Kat absently informed as she finished up with me. "How did he manage to break the big one and only crack the bottom two?"

Molly threw up her hand and shook her head. "I don't know how that man manages to do half the shit he does, but let me tell you, I almost became a widow when he was down."

My eyes got big. "He almost died from a broken leg?"

She laughed and shook her head again. "No, sugar, I almost killed him myself! What a bear!"

She pitched her voice low and gruff. "Molly, bring me the remote. The big one. No, the other big one. Molly, bring me some ice cream. Not that stuff, I want the good stuff. Molly, my back itches. Damn, woman, trim your nails or leave me some skin. Molly, what's for dinner? Don't want meatloaf, want ribs. Molly, I need another movie in the Blu-Ray. Not that one."

She rolled her eyes and ran her hands over her head. "'Bout drove me insane! I'd slip him a couple of those Tylenol PMs once in a while to knock his ass out! Only way I got any peace some days."

They stayed for quite a while, talking and gossiping with me like we were old friends and I wasn't just there as the inconvenient guest. I had a blast. Girl talk was fun, and I could see how great and solid the sisterhood between these women was. All of the old ladies seem to work this way here. Truthfully, I was a bit jealous—this was something I'd never have with my brothers. Yes, we were family and loved each other, but it was just not the same thing.

The pain meds were hitting me and I was starting to drift off when Kat stood up. "I gotta get going. My shift starts in an hour and I need to run a few errands before heading over." She offered me a hand. "Here, I'll help you back to the room."

"I got her," a deep voice uttered, making all three of us jump. Stud came around the back of the couch and set a pair of large cardboard boxes down on the flat coffee table. EVA'S STUFF was marked across one and CACTUS was marked across the other. I had been complaining about having nothing to do except binge-watch Netflix. When Stud was at the Lair, he spent his time with me watching TV as well. We had been back to what we were before the pool party and my accident. We bantered and discussed different actors, films, likes and dislikes, and whatever else came up. As much as I liked the company, that shit was still getting old. I was used to being active, and the enforced bed rest was driving me crazy enough, I asked Stud to sneak in my sewing stuff just as soon as he could. I needed something to occupy by hands before I went totally bonkers!

He bent over and slipped his arms under my legs and behind my back. "Nice duck pants, Cactus. I think I got everything you asked for, but you can check the boxes later. You'll go out like a light once you settle back in the bed," he said, grunting a little as he lifted my weight carefully. I was not a little woman and I knew it was taking him some effort to lift me, however, he did. My ribs protested a bit, but his careful handling helped.

"I *can* walk, you know!" I snapped a little testily. His clean scent teased my nostrils and I so wanted to lay my head on his shoulder and burrow into him.

"Not necessary and the less stress, the faster you'll heal," he said, walking down the hallway. I waved at the departing ladies as they called out their goodbyes. I was very aware of the power of the man holding me so close. And even more aware that he had a bird's-eye view of my boobs as the robe gap showed I was wearing only a thin tank top underneath. It was hard to put on a bra with my bruised ribs, so I had gotten into the habit of leaving it off. I supposed I should have felt uncomfortable or intimidated, but really, I felt… well, I felt warm, secure. Like I was protected. I was sure the happy pills the doctor had prescribed had something to do with the warm and fuzzy feelings. It was weird but temporary, so I'd just enjoy it while I could.

My head did drop down to his shoulder for a moment before he placed me on the bed and slipped his arms out from under me in a slow caress. He pitched a blanket over my legs before sitting next to my hips and placing his arm on the opposite side, effectively caging me in. He leaned over me and stroked my hair back from my face with a light touch that framed my cheek. My lady parts were singing, and my head was spinning with confusion. *Nope, just the happy pills. Nothing more.*

"I got your stuff and made sure no one saw your machine or your materials. Connor helped me get it all together and out. I don't think they would have noticed anyway since they are working nearly round the clock to stay on schedule. It's supposed to rain tonight so Patrick and Angus want to come up here and hang with you for a bit later. Is that okay? Personally, I'd still like to punch both of them out for putting you in this situation."

His fingers kept stroking through my hair. It really felt good. Not just the attention, but the fact he had considered my wishes and done what he could to fill them. That seldom happened in my life. I hummed at the thought of Stud kicking my brothers' asses.

"If you ever do, I wanna front row seat. It's okay with me if they come up later. It's kinda weird not seeing them every day."

He kept stroking. "You've got a real eye and an incredible talent for design. The bar you made for Betsey is beautiful and the inspector said the work was top notch. From what I see, you're way underappreciated by your father and your family. You work nonstop and take a lot of abuse for it when plenty of other companies would give their eyeteeth to have someone like you on their crew. The accident was senseless and could've easily been prevented if any one of your brothers would have stepped up to the plate and done their job. I cannot figure out why you stay."

His question was valid, and I'd be lying if I didn't ask myself that every time Da had a fit or Patrick and Angus pranked me. I was drifting pretty hard under his hand and my eyes were closing. "I don't have a deep-thinking answer for ya. It's jus' my family. S'all I know, and it's all I've ever known."

His hands felt wonderful and I could have stayed there forever under his gentle touch. "Go on and sleep, Cactus. I'll be here when you wake up."

I vaguely felt his lips press to my forehead before I was out.

CHAPTER TWELVE

I'd been at the Lair for nearly three weeks, when Connor came to talk to me. Betsey had insisted that I stay there instead of moving back into my tiny house to finish my recovery. I'd always been a fast healer and was getting around pretty well. My ribs no longer hurt, and my leg was better although it still ached when I pushed it too much.

Connor looked like warmed-over shit. I knew he was pushing himself hard to finish this job as Da had overbooked us again. Since I'd been down for the count for the last month and a half, Connor had called in a few temporary helpers despite Da's protest about paying more people. Connor managed to overrule him, but I know the budget was tight and even though we weren't hurting financially, we still didn't have a giant pot of gold at the end of the rainbow.

"We have to split the crew for a bit, *a stóirín*," Connor said, his tone and stance serious. He sounded tired, probably from working too many hours and dealing with Da's recent screw-ups. I got the feeling this was another one. "We've pushed as hard as we can, but the job in Wilmington overlaps this one by about a week. We need to send a couple of us to the new location to get set up and started, chiefly Da and I. We have enough tools to divide among the two sites for now. Patrick, Angus, Owen, and Garret will stay here and finish. Da and I will go to Wilmington to set up. I've already made some inquiries about temp help to at least clear the new job site, but the budget is very tight and doesn't include money for hotel rooms. You've got another week or two before you're cleared for work again, and you'll still not be at full capacity for a while yet." He jammed a hand over his long face with an air of defeat floating around him. "Ah, Christ, it pains me to ask this, but can me and Da take your house to Wilmington and use it until the others get there with the RV?"

I sat back in the bed. My house? Really? My sanctuary, my space, my stuff, my secrets? My brother wanted me to give that up? Rage flew through me and my head throbbed. How dared he even ask that of me?

"Am I supposed to bunk in the RV?" I croaked. My head really did hurt.

Connor shook his head and gave a grunting laugh. "You'll stay here. Betsey overheard me an' Da arguing about this and she said you're to stay put until you were ready to go. I may be able to argue with Da, but there's no way I'm gonna take on that woman. You can take the train or bus out to us in Wilmington in a couple of weeks. We should be well ready for you by then."

He looked so tired and overwhelmed, I softened. I knew he was dealing with so much bullshit and splitting the crew didn't help. It really was time for Da to retire and let Connor take over. He'd been wanting to expand for years, hiring different people, sending out multiple crews on jobs, subcontracting when possible, making life a little less hectic and a little easier on all of us, but until Da forgot his blasted stubbornness, he was stuck. More than once, I thought Connor would just quit and go do his own thing. I think he stayed on all these years because of our crazy brothers and me.

"Yeah, I guess you and Da can take my house." I took a breath to calm down. "Just please—you know—"

"I'll take care of it," he said, knowing what I was saying without me saying it out loud.

***

"I didn't realize how many hours were in a day until I was forced to sit for so many of them," I said casually to the other ladies. I was sitting at the Lair a week after the RV rolled out with my brothers. By some miracle of nature, they had finished the River's Edge job earlier than expected and left just as soon as they could. Connor and Da were already setup in the North Carolina coastal city of Wilmington and anxiously awaiting their arrival. Connor was texting me daily with updates and asking about my health. Molly, Kat, and Tambre were hanging out with me, oohing and ahhing over the short stack of lap quilts I had folded and piled on the coffee table in front of me. Sometimes they came in shifts, and sometimes all together.

Stud had become my constant companion, showing up in the morning, staying with me all day, and leaving at night either for band rehearsal or for a gig or for his condo if it was not rented for the week. If he was free from band obligations, he'd spend his time with me, joking, laughing, talking, and debating movie buddies. We argued more over who was the best James Bond and went on a movie marathon where we watched them all, a different one every night. Sometimes we were in the Lair's main room with other Dragon Runners around, and sometimes we stayed back in his room, our eyes on his TV screen and me snuggled up against his warm body. He still paid close attention to my injuries, bringing me pain pills and helping me move around. I supposed I should've been annoyed at his hovering, but I kinda liked it. It was nice to have a big strapping man around at times. Not once did I hear gossip about or see him with another woman.

I'd been at the Lair for over six weeks, nearly seven now, and my life had become routine. I got up and did my shower thing, which was difficult and painful at first, but there was no way I was letting Stud help me with that. Next was food. Stud could cook! This was a great thing as I didn't have a lot of skill in that area. I could microwave with the best of them, but real cooking was limited in a tiny house, so I never had an opportunity to do much of it. Betsey would come into the kitchen and chat about the day, her grandkids, the wedding, and would rush out to do whatever it was she had to do. Stud and I then would settle in for the morning's workload. Most often he would be at one of the sitting tables at the Lair, working on his computer, and I'd be working at my sewing machine, stitching up the next project I had started. The silence was broken only by the sounds of my machine or Stud's key clicks.

One or more of the old ladies came by for lunch, either bringing it or making it there. I felt like I was getting waited on hand and foot. I hated it, but like Stud had pointed out time after time, the faster I recovered, the faster I could back get on my feet.

"I've had those days too," Molly sympathized, nodding in agreement. She'd brought sandwiches from a local deli. "There are times I work my ass off all day, then look at the clock and discover I've only been at it a few hours and it ain't even close to closing time. Sucks monkey butt!"

Kat giggled at Molly's complaint. "Could be worse. You could have bedpan duty."

I laughed a bit while snipping some loose threads.

"You're a fantastic seamstress, Eva," Kat said. "I was thinking of asking you this, but you can say no if you want. No hard feelings if you don't want to. Not a problem."

I looked at the timid woman who had befriended me. "I can't say yes or no until I know what you want."

She bit her lower lip, pulling at it between her teeth. "Do you think you can sew me a dress for my wedding? I haven't found anything I really like at the stores, and the one I tried to buy online didn't fit at all. I ended up shipping it back. I'll buy the fabric and stuff and pay you for—"

"I'll do it!" I interrupted. "No charge, this will be my gift to you." I was flattered she thought enough of my work to want to wear it. I'd never sewn for anyone else and was really excited about the idea. I supposed I should have been intimidated, but I wasn't.

"Your lap quilts are beautiful, and I wouldn't mind a couple pairs of your lounge pants. I bet you could sew up table runners, tablecloths, napkins, and that sort of thing pretty easily. If you ever want to sell anything you make, there's Psalm Kopolove's store in town, Soap-n-stuff. She takes a lot of consignment from local artists and craftsmen. They seem to do pretty well. The tourist season here is pretty long with the folks coming in for the train. You should check it out." Tambre spoke quietly while fingering the finished edge of the quilt I was cleaning up.

Tambre was referring to the Great Smoky Mountain Railway, one of the big attractions for this part of the state and a major source of income for many people in the area. Locals referred to it as "that damn train," but many had businesses that thrived on the tourists the railway brought in. The thought of selling my work was another one I hadn't really considered, but it was a good one. I had a small stash of different sized quilts already made during my forced convalescence, and it wouldn't take too long to make the lounge pants or any of the other linens that Tambre suggested. The idea of getting money for my stuff was definitely appealing.

"How would I go about that? Just talk to Psalm?" I asked, folding the finished quilt.

"She has a standard contract she uses," Stud's voice said close enough to my ear. I jumped. I tilted my head back to spot him standing right behind me, arms leaning on the couch cushions and his hand bracketing my shoulders. He looked a bit like a guard dog. I visualized him in a studded collar. He would look really hot.

Damn it! Wrong kind of image!

"There's another street festival coming up. Always something going on in the summer. Be a good way to see if your stuff would sell. 'Specially them lounging pants. I'm gonna want me some as well!" Molly said, coming up on her knees on the couch. She clapped her hands in excitement. "You should totally do this, girlfriend! Can you get her set up, Stud?"

Stud put a warm hand on my shoulder, and I tilted my head back again. His blue eyes met my green ones.

"You want to try this, Eva?" he asked, his voice so low I felt it rumble through me.

I met his gaze straight on. "Yes, I think I do."

He nodded. "Talk to Psalm and see if she has space. I'll print off a blank contract for you. I gave her legal advice and helped her with it. It's as straightforward as you can get. The bones of it is she takes in approved pieces for consignment for a thirty-day limit, no fees. If the piece sells, she takes 20 percent. If the piece stays past thirty days, she charges a storage and display fee, or the seller has the option of removing it. She also takes pictures and puts the pieces up on her store website. Same thirty-day rules and percentages. She collects and takes care of sales taxes. Shipping, income tax, any other fees, that sort of thing are the seller's responsibility. She notifies of sales and pays total sales amount at the end of the month. If the seller wants to know daily or weekly sales, it's up to them to make contact. Make sense?"

Wow! That was a lot of information! Stud just went total lawyer on me, and I liked it. He really did know his stuff, and even though we'd had some ups and downs, I felt I could trust him, at least with this kind of thing.

His phone started ringing and he slipped it from his back pocket only to frown at the number and swipe it closed. He moved away from the couch, saying he'd get the contract and go pick up three or four of my lap quilts from my house. I was to get a few pairs of my lounge pants finished up and call Psalm about setting up an appointment.

"The street festival starts Friday night. If we get your quilts approved today, maybe Psalm can get them set up in the store before then and you'll both get a chance to see buyers' reactions," he said, handing me the paper, still warm from the printer.

Stud had explained the contract, but I read through it anyway. After I talked to Psalm, I would sign my name. I felt a buzz in my gut as I skimmed through the fancy legal language. This was something outside of being a construction worker for my family. This would be something completely mine. Da wouldn't be happy if I left the crew for something different, and I suppose that's the one reason I've stuck around so many years. I knew Connor would be cool with it. Both of us had talked more than once about our lives, how much of it was invested in the family business, and how much we wanted to break away for something else. It was a bit scary thinking that this could actually happen. I'd been programmed to work as a member of the Pub Builders crew since birth, and this sewing consignment thing would be for just me. I supposed I should have been intimidated that the idea of doing something outside my family business could be real, but I found myself excited about it.

"This is a good thing, Eva. Psalm is a good woman, and her

store does really well. Get your stuff together, and I'll take care of business and let you know what she says later today."

Molly shooed him off as only she could do. "Well, go on with ya! We got other things to talk about, like this wedding dress we're gonna design and make."

I raised my eyebrows. I knew Molly sewed, but I didn't know her work, other than pictures of the Catwoman costume she'd made for Kat last Halloween. That sleek design would never be mistaken for a wedding dress!

"What's this 'we' thing, *kemosabe*?" I asked. "Kat asked *me* to sew her dress."

Molly flipped up her hand. "You sew, I design. We'll make a good team."

"Jesus." Stud rolled his eyes and shook his head. "Good luck, Cactus. You too, Kat. Only the good Lord knows what Molly the mischievous will come up with."

His phone rang again, and he looked at it with a harsh scowl before swiping it off a second time. I'd seen Stud happy and smiling, playing music with his band. I'd seen Stud laughing and relaxed, joking around about movies during our Netflix times. I'd seen Stud serious and professional in his dealings with the bar construction and his other accounting work. We'd had deeper conversations about politics, religion, and a bunch of other subjects. The man was brilliant! I'd not seen him with any club women since my accident, and he spent his daily free time being with me in some fashion. I'd even seen him angry and annoyed, but this was different. This phone call was putting him on edge like I'd never seen, and he was tense enough to turn coal into diamonds. Something was wrong, and it was making me worry about him. "I need to run," he said, bending over and kissing the top of my head. "Get those pants ready, babe." He left the room with the contract in his hand.

Tambre clicked her tongue. "Poor man," she said softly as she shuffled through the stack of quilts I had piled up on the coffee table.

"His parents?" Kat asked. Even Molly got quiet and thoughtful.

"They're at it again," Tambre started. "He told Betsey his grandmother is turning ninety next weekend and there's a big party planned for it. He's torn up, wanting to see her but not wanting to see his other family. Still a lot of bad feelings for whatever went down."

I remembered the ladies talking about this a bit at the pool party, but they hadn't given up a lot of detail. "Must have been really bad for him to have turned his back on them," I said casually. "My brothers drive me up the freakin' wall most of the time and I'm mad as hell two of them put me on this couch, but I can't imagine life without them."

Tambre examined several folded pieces of cloth for me to see. "I like these the best for your lounge pants for Psalm. The colors are bright, and the patterns are cute."

I thought she was changing the subject, but I was hoping my

lead-in statement would get her to share more. She did.

"Stud has a mom and dad, brother and sister-in-law, back in Raleigh. They had a bad falling out before he showed up here. To my knowledge, he hasn't spoken to his parents or brother since. He still keeps in touch with his grandma, but that's it. He was messed up for a long time when he was prospecting with the Runners, and I think that's why he took to the club so quick. This brotherhood is more family to him than his own blood. Stud is a strong man, a smart man, but deep down, he's still a hurting man."

She reached for a white-red-and-gold-patterned lap quilt and unfolded it.

"Not my place to get into a brother's business, but if he goes to his grandma's party, and I think he will, he'll need someone at his back. Not right to take a brother in this situation. He best be takin' a sister." She looked at me, making her point abundantly clear. "I like this one the best," she said, making eye contact with the other two women.

I heard Stud's boots echoing down the hallway and all of us started chattering away about wedding colors and dress patterns. As much as these women liked to gossip about the club members, the townsfolk, and whatever else hit their heads, they were fierce as wildcats in the protection of their men. Not just their old men, but all of them. I realized that in all the conversations I'd had with Stud, he never once mentioned his family in the eastern part of the state.

Yup, I'd talk to Stud, and yup, I'd have his back if he wanted it.

CHAPTER THIRTEEN

was at the Lair just over eight weeks, nearly nine. Eight weeks of being pampered and waited on. Paradise, right? Nope, not even a little. I was the worst patient ever, probably because Stud had appointed himself my nurse. I'd always hated being sick, and since it was never tolerated in my family, the confinement was hard.

I supposed it could have been worse. At night, I had Stud's company or that of the other club members in the main room when Stud was busy with band practice or had a gig. Most of the time I had with Stud, we spent it watching movies, playing cards or video games, teasing back and forth, and talking about whatever was on our minds. We'd grown a lot closer over the last two months, and I'd grown very comfortable with him. He'd touch me often, putting his arm around me to play with my hair while we were curled up in front of the TV. He was free with his attentions in front of the brothers too. Once in a while, he would kiss my cheek or my forehead. Quick, dry affectionate pecks that were more brotherly or friendly. I didn't really want to feel the brother-from-another-mother thing going on with him, but I still liked it.

Things took a turn about a week ago.

It was during the day and I was bored out of my mind, pacing up and down the hallways trying to find something to do. I was out of usable fabric. I had already finished my laundry (and Stud's just so I could keep my hands occupied). The club was moving stuff in, getting set up for the big grand opening for the new River's Edge, and the majority of club members were involved in the work. I was by myself, feeling fine and healing very well, and about to go a bit stir-crazy from the confinement. Fuck my life!

"Babe, you really need to settle," I heard as I wandered back down the long hallway to the main room. Stud was setting up his laptop at his usual spot. He'd been in and out all morning between the Lair and the bar, feeding me limited information. I was not used to being this out of touch and really wanted to see the finished building.

"I can't!" I snapped, flopping down on the couch. "I've been sitting on my ass for weeks now and I'm done with this shit! Everyone is down there helping out and I'm stuck here doing laundry. *Laundry* of all things!" I huffed and crossed my arms, ignoring the slight pull of my ribs.

He looked at me a moment and then unplugged his computer to stow it back in its case. "All right then, go suit up."

"Huh?"

"Go get some different clothes on, Cactus. You've been lounging long enough. Let's go for a ride." He gave me that half smile of his I liked so much.

"You're kidding, right?" I asked.

"Nope. Get your lazy ass moving, babe. Unless you don't want to go?"

I nearly broke my ribs again scrambling off the couch. Ten minutes later, we were out at his bike and he was handing me a helmet.

He checked the straps under my chin. "There's a radio. All you have to do is speak normally and I'll hear you. If you start hurting, let me know. Okay?"

"I got it, big guy, let's go already!" I was super stoked to be riding on a bike again.

We made the short ride to the River's Edge bar in no time. It kinda sucked, as I was ready for more, but seeing the completed project took the sting away.

It was beautiful, one of our best. Rustic cabin exterior, stone chimney set that would look great in the winter with smoke curling from its top, and plenty of paved parking met my eyes. Inside was bustling as pictures and the neon bar sign were being hung, tables, chairs, and benches were being moved and set in place by the men. The Runners had even commissioned new chainsaw-art bar stools that looked fantastic lined up against the bar I had designed. Betsey was directing the whole show.

"Lord have mercy, child! What are you doing here and why in the Sam Hill did you ride that bike? You sure you're ready for that?" she barked, hugging me and scolding me at the same time.

"I'm not used to being still for so long, Betsey. Couldn't take it anymore. Don't get mad at Stud. I made him bring me down."

She rolled her eyes and made her irritated *pshht* sound. "Well as long as you're here, what do you think? The inspector was right pleased at the level of the work. Y'all did a great job!"

Yeah, we did. I thought proudly.

We chatted for a bit while Stud checked in with Brick and some of the other club men. I saw him reach for his phone at one point and frown deeply at the number, but instead of swiping it closed, he answered it and walked off to be by himself. Betsey saw it as well.

"Oh Lord, here it comes," she said in a resigned tone. "If you have a praying bone in your body, please send up all you can to the man upstairs. Stud needs all the help he can get if he goes back to that viper den."

I didn't get a chance to answer as I watched Stud ram the phone into his back pocket and stride toward us.

"You feeling okay?" he asked me, his mouth in a thin line. "Wanna ride a bit longer? Maybe the Tail for a short run?"

"Yup! I'm feeling so good I expect I'll get taxed on it!" I grinned at him, hopefully to offset whatever made him lose his good mood. It didn't work.

He handed me my helmet and strapped his back on. I waved at Betsey as we pulled out, taking in her concerned face and giving her a thumbs-up. I hoped she was reassured at least a little for both my condition and Stud's.

A little while later, we passed the marker noting the start of the Tail of the Dragon.

Stud had been steering carefully and I felt the growling machine under me bulge with power, wanting to open up and fly. When we came onto the Tail, I heard Stud talk to me through the tinny-sounding radio.

"Are you still good? No pain in the leg or ribs? I'd like to open up a bit but not if you're hurting."

My answer was to get a better grip around his middle, resting my hand on his lower stomach and pressing against his back.

"'Bout time you showed me how a real biker rides! Let's go!" I answered back.

"You let me know if it's too much." He took off. I felt a jerk but nothing serious enough for me to complain about.

I really, *really* needed one of these in my life! Riding bitch to

Stud was great, but I so wanted to feel what it was like to ride and control one of these beasts. We took the curves and I felt a pull but no pain in the force. I leaned with Stud into each turn, feeling his body communicate how far to go and when to stop. He was magnificent in his control and command of the bike. I felt tingly all over thinking about what he could do if he had command and control over me. It was hard nixing that thought. Hey, I could still dream a little, right?

He crested a hill, then pulled over to a scenic outlook. A family with two little boys was also there, taking pictures and letting the kids run around a bit. Stud barely glanced at them as he parked the bike and took off his helmet.

"Look at the motorcycle!" I heard one boy, maybe around six years old, say to his brother as I dismounted. He pointed at us, his eyes full of wonder at the shiny big toy. The other one, young enough to still be in diapers, just sat in the dirt and poked a grubby finger up his nose. The parents cast a few wary looks in our direction but kept away.

Stud practically ripped the helmet off and nearly pitched it to the ground before roughly jamming it on the rest designed to hold it. I took mine off and stowed it next to his. He stomped off to the stone fence that was more pretty than protection at the edge of the overlook. The scene was gorgeous! Big clear blue sky over a richly green forest, a few wisps of clouds, clean air, and an eagle soaring high overhead. I wished Stud could see what I saw, but he seemed too into his own head.

I smiled at the boys and stepped over to Stud, placing a hand on his back and rubbing it absently over his cut and up to his neck. His hair was pulled back in a ponytail and slightly sweaty from the ride, stress, or both. I could feel the tension in his shoulders. I wanted to comfort him somehow, but not knowing what was in his head didn't help much. I just stood next to and slightly behind him with my hand on his hot neck, hopefully transferring some of my strength to him.

He turned and faced me, his look intense and unreadable. My hand fell away as I stared into the deep blue of his eyes.

"Did you sleep with Table?" he ground out, fists at his sides as if trying to control them.

I blinked in surprise. Of all the things I expected him to say, that wasn't one of them.

"What?" I asked, screwing up my nose. Did I really hear him right?

"Did. You. Sleep. With. Table?" he asked again, his voice rough and firm. He moved a step closer to me.

Was I or was I not Eva MacAteer? "Of course not, you asshole!" I yelled, punching at his shoulders with both fists. "I've never slept with *anyone*, and it ain't looking real good for you right now!"

He stepped back from the force of my angry shove and blinked. "You're a virgin?"

Gah! Did I really just shout that bit of personal information out loud?

"Is that a crime? Think about it, genius! I have five older brothers and a dad who I'm with nearly 24/7. When the hell do you think I'm gonna find the time or place or even a man willing to take all of them on? I'm surprised as fucking hell they've not noticed or given me grief about you coming over so much!"

"They're not saints, Eva. I've seen them around with the club women and others from the town."

"Yeah well, chauvinism and double standards are alive and well in my family." I was boiling mad, at both his insinuations and his own chauvinistic attitude. "Who the fuck do you think you are to judge me and my life? You're not exactly lily-white yourself!" I went to shove him again. I was seeing red in fiery hues and colors. Stud had other ideas.

He grabbed me and slammed me hard into his body. His mouth came down on mine, kissing me into silence. His tongue swept inside when I protested. I thought briefly about biting him, as I was still mad, but instead I kissed him back with as much fervor as he kissed me. I felt my breasts tighten and my lady parts sing. He slowed down and softened his touch, tasting and exploring my mouth, sucking at my lower lip, before dipping in again and again. I was one big ball of need. His hands came down and grabbed my ass, lifting me high and grinding against me. I could feel his hardness through our jeans and wished there was nothing between us. This was what I wanted. Him inside me.

Like a sudden cold shower, I heard a small high-pitched voice yell out, "Mom! Look!"

Dammit! I had completely forgotten we had an audience. I guess they just got an earful as well as an eyeful. Stud pulled back and rested his forehead against mine. Both of us were breathing hard, still wrapped up in each other. I could hear the sudden slam of the van's doors as the family quickly departed. It almost made me want to laugh, but with Stud's hand still on my ass and the other buried in my hair, laughter wasn't the best idea.

We stayed that way for a long time, just breathing and feeling. A light wind blew in random puffs around us, whistling quietly and cooling.

"I'm sorry, Eva. You're absolutely right. I'm not a saint either and have no right to judge you or your life. I hope you can forgive me. Table is my brother and you'd be hard pressed to find a better man. He would be a great partner, but the thought of you and him together rips into my gut like a knife. I don't ever want him in your bed. I want *me* in your bed, and I hope to God you'll someday find me worthy of it."

My brain reeled from his words. What did I do with this? I didn't have an Eva persona to pull out and deal. No witty comebacks or snarky sentences came to my mind. What I did know was I wanted more kisses. More Stud. Just more.

"I don't know what to say," I breathed. "I'm not with Table. Not then, and obviously not now."

"Will you come with me to Raleigh this weekend?" he asked, his voice quiet. "My grandmother is the one person who means something to me in the family there and the only one I still talk to. I'll be blunt, Eva, in that I don't give a shit about the others, but she called me and asked me herself to come. I was going to go alone, but I'd rather have you with me. I think I need you with me."

What could I say? There was only one answer.

"Yes."

CHAPTER FOURTEEN

Plans were quickly made. **We** would ride Stud's bike and after the party Stud would drive me to Wilmington to meet up with my family and resume my life. I wasn't real sure that's what I wanted, but it was a plan and made sense at the time. Thank God for the club women or else we never would have been able to pull this off with such a short time frame. Molly helped me sew a new dress, while Tambre and Betsey got my stuff packed into shipping boxes. They were sent to the hotel jobsite where Connor had setup, and he would keep my stuff until I got there. The trip to Stud's family place would only be for one night, so I didn't have to pack a lot for it. My return to my life was quicker than I expected, and I was really down about leaving the Dragon Runners, but no matter what, I was going to keep my ties with these people who had come to mean so much to me. I would be back at least for Kat and Mute's wedding.

We had ridden the bike nearly five hours to get to Stud's family home. My butt was numb, and I knew I would be a bit sore as I still had some twinges going on in my ribs and leg, but I was tough. I perked up when we rode through a fancy-schmancy neighborhood with big houses. Nope. Not houses. Mansions. Maybe even more like estates. With lots of land around man-made lakes. As a builder, I could appreciate the tall columns and creative architecture, and what kind of army it took to keep those lawns in showplace condition. As Eva, I thought *what the fuck have I gotten myself into?*

Stud pulled up to a fancy iron gate and pressed a number code into the security pad at the side. The gates clicked and we rode into a landscaped courtyard. It was painfully overdone. The flowers and shrubs were ranked and sculpted into geometric forms, appearing rigid and under such absolute control they couldn't grow in any direction or place other than at the desire of the gardener. No unauthorized growth or weed would dare show itself and ruin the perfect lines and color scheme. It looked plastic. I had the urge to pick a flower just to see if some garden gnome would come and arrest me.

As we cruised the paved circular drive, I could feel the tension start in Stud's back. He'd stopped talking to me several miles outside of the city and I knew he wasn't happy. I'd seen so many different Studs. Happy, goofy, flirty, mad, determined, but so far, I'd never seen him dark.

I turned my attention to the house. Marble steps leading up to an impressive set of elaborately carved oak doors with heavy brass knockers, and they opened on a whisper as we pulled up and a man dressed in formal attire appeared.

"Master Beauregard, how nice to see you again, sir. We've made space in the garage for your—ah—vehicle. Shall I call a chauffeur to take it there?" he stated in a dry monotone voice. Obviously, this guy was the head butler, and just as obviously, he didn't like either Stud or me at the moment.

Stud took off the helmet and shook out his long mane, almost in defiance. "No thanks, Jameson. I'll take it later." He slipped on his mirrored aviators, perhaps to shield himself from the bright afternoon sun, but more likely to hide his unrest.

I could feel the butler's disapproval radiating down his arrogant thin nose. "Very well then. Luncheon is being served in thirty minutes on the small veranda. I'll show your—ah—lady friend to her room. You, of course, sir, have your same chambers."

Hmmm—Stud has chambers and I got a room. I didn't know how I felt about that.

Stud dismounted after me and stretched his arms back. Experienced biker or not, it was a long trip. "I can show her, Jameson."

"Mrs. Franklin decided to put your—friend—in the green room." The disdain was unmistakable. I was starting to get pissed. Who the hell did this guy think he was?

The mirrored glasses jerked up to the pretentious man. "I specifically requested Eva be placed in the blue room near mine."

"Mrs. Franklin thought it best otherwise." The man practically sniffed.

I could see Stud's jaw tighten up. Uh-oh! *Time to make it real, Eva.*

I took off my helmet and shook out my hair as well. I also reached down and grabbed double handfuls of my ass and began massaging. "Green, blue, purple, orange, or pink, I really don't give a shit as long as it's got a rack and a head." I was fake as hell, but I got a twitch out of Stud's upper lip. "My ass went numb passing through Burlington, and I could use a change of clothes. Lead the way, J-man!"

Jameson's thin eyebrows seemed to disappear into his receding hairline. He stared at me as if he expected my head to start spinning around.

"Very well. Right this way." His stiff movements were hilarious.

I leaned over and whispered in Stud's ear, "Does Mr. Roboto run on a battery pack or do they plug him in every night?"

Stud burst into laughter and hugged me close, his whole demeanor relaxed at least for the moment.

If the butler was bad, lunch with his mother was worse. After we dropped off our packs in our rooms, Jameson led us to a nice covered veranda that overlooked another meticulously sculpted and painfully landscaped lawn. The grass was cut in uniform stripes, the flower beds arranged with colors and plants forced into more unnatural shapes and designs. I supposed it was pretty in a way, but I still found it cold and fake.

Stud's mom really rounded that idea out perfectly.

"Beauregard," a female voice greeted him.

I turned and saw an older, female version of Stud walking toward us. Thin and beautiful, she was definitely the Southern queen of her Southern kingdom. She was wearing a pale pink dress that came to just below her knees, low-heeled pumps, full makeup, and pearls. She looked younger than I expected, but since her face didn't move much I suspected Botox or plastic surgery. Maybe both.

"Abigail," Stud returned. *Wait? Who calls their mom by her first name?*

The regal woman offered her hand and tilted her head. Stud dutifully gave her a light kiss on her pale white cheek. It was one of the most choreographed moves I'd ever seen. The Jameson robot thing made sense now. Stud's mom was an alien.

"You're looking well. It's very nice of you to come to your grandmother's party. I trust your journey was pleasant?" she inquired stiffly.

"It was fine," Stud replied. "This is Eva MacAteer."

He gestured for me to come forward and meet his alien mom.

"Nice to meet you, Eva," she said in a tone that said it was anything *but* nice.

We sat down to a white wicker outdoor table with so many twists and scrolls, it was more artwork than functional. There were white china place settings so thin and delicate, I was afraid to touch anything. Ranked next to the plates were way more forks and spoons than I had fingers. At least I knew what do to with the napkin. I looked at Stud who was wearing a stiff face, clearly not happy with this scene.

"This wasn't necessary, Abigail," he said in a low, cold voice. Nope. Stud was not happy.

"Nonsense, Beauregard. I should always want to put out the best for my oldest son, even though he never deigns to visit me." I noticed she said nothing about putting out the best for any guest he may bring. "Besides, Danforth and Vanessa will be joining us."

I'd way underestimated Stud's feelings—to say he was simply unhappy was a total mistake. The heat from his rage poured off him in waves.

"What the fuck makes you think I would ever want *them* joining us?"

Abigail's hand fluttered to her neck. "My word, Beauregard! Your language! Is this what you've learned by being with those—people?"

I wanted to bring out Smartass Eva to help defuse the situation and get Stud laughing again, but she was too busy getting angry herself at the snobbish remark.

As quick as that, Stud's mom relaxed her posture and face, and again appeared to be the regal queen of her kingdom.

"Oh, and here they are now!" She rose and stepped forward to greet a man and a woman who had just walked onto the veranda.

The man looked like Stud in the face, but that's where it stopped. His hair was cut, styled, and slicked in place. He wore an expensive-looking gray suit with a matching tie and pocket square. His shoes were tooled leather and looked expensive as well. He had the soft, pale look of a desk jockey.

The woman was a classic beauty, almost cookie cutter of Abigail. She had long blonde hair artfully done up in a fancy French twist and wore a plain pale yellow dress that fitted her like a glove, showing off a perfect figure. My first impression of her was porcelain doll more than Barbie lookalike, but Barbie still qualified.

I was still in my travel clothes of old jeans, tank top, and tennis shoes. Pretty big contrast, and I couldn't say I wasn't bothered by it, but there wasn't anything I could do. Besides, Stud was more important and that's who I was here for.

"Now that we're all here, we can begin," Abigail trilled lightly. "Jameson, we are ready."

Mr. Roboto helped Abigail into her seat and moved to seat Vanessa as well. He didn't look like he was moving in my direction, so I plopped down in the closest chair. Abigail raised her perfectly plucked eyebrows but said nothing. The men seated themselves and I was glad to have Stud next to me. I couldn't quite call him Beauregard yet, but planned on teasing him later. I hoped I would get at least a half smile out of that.

Lunch was just as fancy looking as the garden. A waiter appeared in a black and white uniform, carrying a tray of little plates with little cantaloupes. They were cut out at the tops like crowns and filled with chicken salad topped with a circle of chopped celery pieces, red grapes, and chia seed sprinkles. Parsley sprigs and a lemon wedge decorated the edge of the plate. It looked like the fake food that gets set up by real estate people at one of those open houses, trying to entice people to buy. Too pretty to eat and with the array of forks in front of me, I wasn't quite sure how!

No one was moving to start. Danforth was tapping on his phone. Stud had told me the names of his family members and mentioned he had a younger brother, but this guy looked older with bags under his eyes and deep lines around his mouth. He was a lawyer also and had taken a partnership in the family's law firm. He had nodded in Stud's direction but neither man had spoken a greeting nor even shaken hands. The only info I got on Vanessa was being Danforth's wife. Stud clammed up tight after speaking her name.

Abigail and Vanessa were making small talk about the party, the arrangements, hair appointments, and other such bits. They were pointedly ignoring me. Stud was sitting stiffly, and I watched his hands clench and unclench on his thighs. Definitely time for Smartass Eva. I leaned over to Stud and loudly whispered in his ear, "Papa John's come out this way? I gotta coupon code we can use."

He burst into laughter, head back and mouth open. Mission accomplished. I smiled at him, finally relaxing. He tagged me at the back of my neck, pulled me in, and kissed me lightly.

"Love you, Cactus," he said, before grabbing the biggest fork and digging up a massive scoop of the chicken salad.

All three of his family members visibly froze, first at his loud laugh and then at his words. I managed to cover my reaction to his words by grabbing my biggest fork too and shoveling a big bite into my mouth. Nah. He was just talking, like when you say you love steak or love to go fishing. I glanced up and caught Vanessa staring at me with an unreadable look. Disdain maybe? Regret? Envy? No matter. I was not planning on ever seeing these people again after this weekend. I'd gladly take another sore ass from a long trip to get out of this place come tomorrow morning. Abigail just looked at me like I was a bug that crawled across the table. I forked up more chicken salad. It was actually pretty good.

Stud moved me to the blue room he wanted me in by taking my pack there himself and daring Jameson to say something. I thought Mr. Roboto's eyebrows would take root in his hairline. He didn't protest, however, just an eye twitch as he left us alone. I managed to nap a bit, laid out on the ginormous bed. The blue room connected to Stud's "chambers" via a shared bathroom. We "lower sort" call that a jack and jill. I bet the upper crust call it something else.

Later that night, I sat before the antique vanity table and stroked the last coat of mascara over my lashes, leaning back to check the final results. My eyes looked bigger and brighter with the silver and smoke colored eye shadows Molly had found for me at Psalm's shop. However, instead of curling my hair and teasing it into a big halo as she had suggested, I ironed it flat and let it hang straight down my bare back like a shimmering curtain. My dress, I had designed for me and my body. Molly let me raid her fabric closet for the material, and with her help in cutting and fitting, I was able to finish it in a day. The halter-style top fastened around my neck leaving my shoulders, back, and arms bare. This showed off my hard body quite well. The long skirt came just below my ankles and was slightly A line, making my body long and lithe. It had a long front spilt that opened and closed when I walked. The color was a deep forest green that had a light iridescence that shimmered when I moved. I liked my dress and felt really good wearing it. I was still sore from the accident and my thigh ached a bit as I was building my strength back up. I wished I could have worn my fabulous silver Jimmy Choos and maroon LBD, but they were currently in Wilmington with Connor and Da. Thankfully, Molly had a closet full of heels and we were the same size. This was the moment in life I had hoped for, to be Princess Eva. Beautiful Eva.

I didn't really have a name for her as I'd never been her before.

A knock on the shared door startled me enough to make me jump. I was nervous as hell but trying not to show it. Stud was on edge as well. He was wound tight like a coiled spring, and I thought he would snap at any minute. I hoped Smartass Eva was enough to help him get through the night. I was to meet his grandmother, the only person he really wanted to see and the only reason we'd come to this event.

I heard the door open and Stud filled the frame. My breath stopped for a moment at how he looked. The handsome Viking biker was still there, but decked out in a fitted black tuxedo. He was fastening a cuff link that winked burnished gold. When he turned to close the door, I spotted the gold clasp he used to pull back his hair into a brushed ponytail at the nape of his neck. Jesus, Mary, and Joseph, he was hot! I felt myself flush with color.

"You ready for this, sweetheart?" he asked, meeting my eyes with his. I could drown in the blue.

"Yeah, I'm good," I said, more breathily than I should have. I smiled and stood up. "Let's go see Grandma!"

***

Stud fiddled with his cuff link, trying not to think about Eva and the fact that her bed was only a few feet away. The dress she wore was the stuff of dreams, showing off her curves and her tight body. The slit in the skirt draped back, showing her super toned legs. Many women in this social circle spent hours in the gym with personal trainers and huge amounts of money on plastic surgery to get bodies like Eva's. She simply worked at her job. What was even more amazing was that she didn't even know how beautiful and sexy she was. He'd seen Vannie looking at her earlier during that damnable lunch where his mother had ambushed him. He frowned when he spotted the edge of the still-red scar on her thigh. He knew she would probably be hurting before the night was over, but the woman was damn stubborn.

She stood up from the vanity, her skirt swishing into place and the heels putting her nearly at his height.

"Yeah, I'm good. Let's go see Grandma," she said, her voice low and husky in a way that shot straight to his dick.

Fuck! He was glad she was here. He hadn't realized how much he'd come to enjoy and need her company. He slipped up at lunch and said the "L" word. It startled him that it came out of his mouth as naturally as it had.

He tipped up her chin with an index finger and covered her lips lightly with his, and paused, taking in her taste. Cherry. She was wearing lip balm instead of some expensive designer lipstick. The symbolism was not lost on him.

The kiss was brief and he folded her into his arms, feeling her strength and support blend into his.

"You look stunning, Eva. Thank you for being here with me. I couldn't do this without you," he said, meaning every word.

She squeezed him back, her face soft with meaning. "No problem, Stud. I wouldn't want to be anywhere else tonight but here. Now let's get to this fancy shindig! I'm hungry. Should've got that pizza earlier."

He chuckled and scooped up the gift bag as they left the room. He held her hand on the way down the steps to face the coming stress known as his family.

CHAPTER FIFTEEN

We made our way to the garden where the party was to take place. The fountains were burbling quietly and a string quartet was tuning up at one corner of the veranda. Waiters in black and white were loading up the buffet tables with food trays that looked more like art than food and those big bins that had the little cups of blue flame under them to keep the contents warm. I didn't know what they were called, but I always thought those things looked cool. Strings of lights cast a pretty glow in the fading sun, but nothing could soften the cold, rigid look of the plant beds. I still thought they looked plastic.

Abigail wanted to set up a receiving line to greet the guests who had begun to arrive, and made it clear this was for family only and I wasn't a part of it. I saw Stud burr up for an argument, but I managed to defuse it by saying I needed to sit anyway and give my leg as much rest as possible. My leg was fine, but he bought the story.

"Stay where I can see you," he growled.

I nodded, grabbed a glass of wine from a nearby waiter, and sat at a table on the veranda where Stud had a clear view of me. I put the gift bag down on the table so he could see that too. Tension showed in the tightness of his face and shoulders. He looked at me and gave me a chin lift to ask if I was okay. I rolled my eyes and raised my glass at him. *I'm good. Go play rich people!* As if he heard me, he smiled his half smile, closed his eyes, and shook his head slightly. I hoped I could keep up and survive the night. *Can you say guppy in a shark tank?*

I sipped at the wine, trying not to grimace. Wine has never been my thing, and this one was nasty. Give me a good beer any day over this stuff. Since I knew only one person at the party who would ever talk to me and he was currently occupied, I spent the next bit of time people watching. The men were dressed mostly in tuxes, but a few were in expensive looking suits. I had the feeling these were custom-tailored ones, not the ones my brothers would buy off the rack at a discount warehouse to wear under protest at funerals or weddings. Slicked-back or styled hair, clean-shaven faces; a lot of them looked alike. I imagined they were all rich businessmen, lawyers, doctors, or politicians; a world I would never be a part of.

The women were another story. Glitter? I'd never seen so much sparkle from throats, fingers, and ears. Most of the older women wore long formals and the younger ones were in shorter cocktail dresses. They drifted together, air kissing each other on both cheeks like I'd seen in movies. I did find it odd that this was supposed to be a birthday party for a woman who was turning ninety. The crowd looked more the same age as Stud's parents and younger. It made me wonder whose party this really was.

I turned my attention back to Stud and his family, standing at the garden entrance in family order. There was a huge difference between him and his family. Not in their appearance, as they were all beautiful people. It was deeper. Beauregard Sr. was first, looking every bit the king of his castle. He shook hands and nodded as he greeted the people coming down the line. There was a semi-smile on his face, but not one that reached his eyes. He looked more like this was an obligation than a party for his mother. He had not spoken one word to me since we arrived. Plastic flowers, I thought again. Abigail came next in a conservative beige gown with a boat neck bodice that sparkled with hundreds of glass beads sewn into it, and a draping chiffon skirt that reached the floor but had a slight rise in front so her beige pumps could be seen. I knew this style was chosen mainly so she wouldn't have any problems with tripping or catching the skirt with her shoes. It wouldn't be seemly for the queen to falter, now would it? I noticed that some people she would shake hands with and some she just nodded at politely.

Stud was the odd man out in a lot of ways. He'd finally relaxed and seemed to be enjoying himself. Whenever he recognized someone in the line, he shook hands, smiled genuinely, hugged with a few back slaps, laughed out loud, or all of the above. His ponytail and trimmed beard alone set him apart, but his open behavior outshone the others around him to the point they faded away.

Danforth was a cookie-cutter image of his father. Same tux, same haircut, same look, same nod and handshake, same semi-smile. I needed to remember later to ask Stud if Danforth was really his brother or if he was a clone of his father.

Vanessa stood at the end of the line, looking like an angel in a sleeveless white bandage dress that wrapped around her like a second skin. It was short, coming to about midthigh, and showed off her perfect curves. Her hair was clipped back in a silver and diamond barrette in a fall of gentle blonde curls that draped over her bare shoulders. A single large diamond on a silver chain hung between the tops of her perfect high breasts. Open-toed silver stilettos adorned her perfect feet with toenails tipped in white. Barbie at her finest.

The gauntlet continued as guest after guest came through; Beau Sr.'s nod, Abigail's limp touch, Stud's laugh, Danforth's grunt, and Vanessa's vague smile. Every once in a while, I'd catch Stud's glance and his lifted eyebrow.

You good? he seemed to be asking. I would wink, roll my eyes, or give him a thumbs-up, much to his amusement. The others simply ignored me. I couldn't say I wasn't bothered by their censure, but since I wasn't here to impress them, fuck it. I'd drink this nasty wine, smile a fake smile, and get through the next twelve hours until we could leave for the coast. The first thing I would do when I saw my own family would be to hug the shit out of them and tell them I loved them. That was before punching Patrick and Angus in their faces. I still owed them that for the roof thing.

The line finally petered out and Stud was able to get away. He came straight over to me as I stood up. My thigh burned a little, but I was still determined to make it through the night in my fabulous shoes.

"Glad that's over with," he said, meaning every word. He took my hand and pulled me closer for a brief hug. "Come on and meet the person I really came to see. Bea brought Nana in a few minutes ago by the side gate and got her settled on her throne. She's the one redeeming person here tonight."

He led me down the veranda steps to the covered area off to the side of the stone fountain. A wrinkled elderly lady was sitting in a wheelchair conversing with an equally wrinkled black lady. Stud's grandmother and her caretaker were in complete opposition to the glitz around them and didn't seem to care. The white-haired woman had on navy blue sweatpants and a sweatshirt that stated GO

DUKE! across the chest. Her feet were encased in thick white socks and Keds. The only jewelry she wore was a plain gold band on her left hand. Her caretaker was an older black woman with a head of gray hair who was dressed in sweatpants and a sweatshirt that read GO HEELS! Clearly there was a serious rivalry between the two of them. I smiled as we approached. I could already tell why Stud would deal with his family to see her and be here for her birthday.

"'Bout damn time you came over here!" she barked at Stud when we entered the area. "Get your ass over here, boy, and introduce me to your girlfriend!"

I bit my lip at her demand and waited for Stud to correct her, but he simply laughed and bent to kiss his grandmother on her dry powdery cheek.

"Nana, this is Eva MacAteer. Eva, this is Thelma Franklin, my beloved, cantankerous, stubborn grandmother, and her sidekick Bea Hairston."

"You forgot old. I did turn ninety a few days ago. Didn't want this big hootenanny, but your mother had to have it and your father wanted the connections for Danforth. He's trying to get that cotton head to run for the state senate. Lord knows what will happen if he gets in office."

"Thelma, you ought to be ashamed of yourself, talking like that about your own grandson! And in front of Little Beau's lady friend! What's she gonna think of you?" Bea scolded. Her hands were busy with a crochet hook and were flying as they formed a granny square with an anchor pattern in the middle. I was fascinated by the deftness in her gnarled fingers.

"She's gonna think I'm the only one in this family who hasn't lost their mind. Come sit over here and tell me about yourself," the tiny dynamo demanded, piercing me with her pale blue eyes. "What does your family do and how did you meet my grandson?"

"Nana," Stud breathed in mock warning.

"My family is in construction as in we design and build bars and pubs," I answered as I sat on a white rental chair near the older woman. Stud moved behind me and placed his hands on my bare shoulders. I did my best to ignore the light stroke of his fingers.

"We are the architects and the crew for most of the work. That's how I met Stud. My family just finished rebuilding his club's bar and grill."

Her look was steady. I could see where Stud got his intense focus as well as his gorgeous eyes. "I'm not surprised. You look like you could bench press a horse. Maybe two." Her tone was one of admiration, not derision. "Takes a strong woman to keep my boy in line. What did you call him? Stud?"

I cleared my throat. "Umm—yeah, Stud. It's his club road name and the only one I've ever called him."

"Makes no sense to me why he'd want a name like that. My husband's name was Beauregard. Perfectly fine family name, though it's been a little tarnished now and then. Stud, eh? Probably suits him well. You know when he was a boy, I used to call him my little Bo-Bo. Did he tell you that?"

"Jesus, Nana!" Stud chuckled and turned red. Red! I was so keeping this for later blackmail material.

I bit my lip, trying to hold in the laughter, and shook my head. "No, he didn't. He doesn't talk much about this side of his family."

The old woman snorted. "I can believe that! After the shit they pulled!"

"Now, Thelma! You shouldn't be dragging that mess out here," Bea admonished quietly, her fingers still flying.

I felt Stud go still against my back and his hands stopped their movement. Betsey had alluded to something bad that had happened and now Stud's grandmother mentioned it, too. I expect whatever it was didn't need to come out in the middle of a ninetieth birthday party.

"You're really good at crocheting, Bea. I like the color scheme. What are you making?" I changed the subject quickly.

Bea looked up with a sympathetic and knowing look. This wasn't her first rodeo. "I'm workin' on a new afghan for my youngest grandson. He's getting ready to graduate from high school and just got accepted into Chapel Hill. I've made all my grandbabies afghans when they left home. I'd like to think it keeps them warm and reminds them there's someone that loves them and thinks of them all the time."

My thoughts drifted to Stud's afghan, but I didn't say anything. I wasn't sure if I should admit I'd been in his bedroom.

Bea continued. "Been working all my life. I can't just sit with my hands not busy. Don't matter if it's TV watching or what. Thelma just gives me grief 'bout workin' all the time but I like it, and as long as my fingers still work, Imma gonna keep 'em busy."

Thelma snorted again. "What's in the bag?" she asked, clearly ready to move on.

"I—uh—don't crochet, but I—um—sew." I handed her the plain brown bag. "Sorry for not wrapping it fancier, but since we travelled by bike there wasn't a lot of room."

Bea's hands stopped as she watched her charge pull out and spread open the log cabin lap quilt I'd been working on during my downtime at the Lair. The purple and green strips alternated in layers, showing a block pattern that was both simple and complex at the same time. I'd used a gold border between each larger piece, and extra-thick batting which took quite a while to complete, but would be extra warm and soft.

"You make this, child?" Bea asked, reaching her fingers out to stroke over the material. "Nice even stitches. I bet this took a while."

"I had time," I said, getting a little uncomfortable, but still enjoying the praise. "I understand the need to keep your hands busy."

"Mardi Gras colors," Thelma said as her bent fingers smoothed over the quilt. "My husband and I went there when he was stationed at the naval base in New Orleans. He was a military lawyer, but we didn't have a pot to piss in back then so the best we could do was to go see the parades. I loved it so much! The lights. The colors."

Her eyes twinkled and voice drifted back into the memory. "I earned a lot of beads, let me tell you!"

"Shit, Nana!" I heard Stud say under his breath. I couldn't tell if he admired his grandmother for her boldness or was embarrassed by her admission.

"My good gracious, Thelma Franklin! I cain't believe you showed off your titties in public! For plastic beads that ain't got no value? I say you shoulda held out for cash money!" Bea picked up her crochet needle again, and it started flashing in her nimble hands. "That's a fine-looking quilt, Eva. You done a good job. I'm bettin' you did that dress too, seein' as it's fitted right proper. Has them same tiny stitches."

Stud's fingers tightened on my neck. "Yeah, she made it, Bea. Designed it too." His thumbs caressed my shoulders, both stroking up to the back of my head. I felt a rush of goose bumps prick up as a shot of electricity ran down my spine.

"That's really nice work," Bea intoned, with a sidelong glance at her charge. "Nice to see somethin' other than Duke blue!"

Thelma had been stroking the quilt now spread over her lap. She immediately latched on to the bait.

"Blue Devils over Tarheels any day!" she barked, scowling. "Best

STUD

damn basketball team ever!" she declared.

"Maybe basketball, but we're in football season now. My Tarheels can hold their own against anyone! Been undefeated this year, thanks to my grandson. You're gonna lose big time, you old Blue Devil!"

The women argued back and forth a bit, showing off knowledge of a good number of the teams' statistics from past years and their current records. I could see the affection between them even as they poked at each other. I tilted my head back and caught Stud's amused expression. His attention came to me. "Did you go to Duke or Chapel Hill?" I asked.

"Both. Got my undergrad at UNC Chapel Hill and my law degree from Duke."

"Where did you go?"

It took me a moment to realize Thelma was addressing me. Her piercing look was back.

"I didn't. I've worked in my family business all my life. I got a high school diploma and kept working." I swallowed a bit nervously but didn't back down. If my lack of formal education was a problem, it was hers and not mine.

She nodded. "We used to call that the school of hard knocks. Some folks would benefit from taking those lessons rather than a four-year degree in something like art appreciation. Least if you choose art you need to be an artist, not just appreciate it!"

Stud cleared his throat like he was stifling himself.

"Now tell me something, Eva. This is really important for anyone who's with my grandson. Devils or Heels?" Her eyes bored into mine and she wore a serious scowl on her face, like my answer was going to determine life or death.

"Neither," I said. "My family is Irish so there's only one team worth anything," I stated with as much seriousness as I could manage. "Go Notre Dame!"

She slowly blinked. Then her face cracked into a wide smile and she seemed to burst. She clapped her hands together in her lap and threw her head back, laughing loud and real. I could see why Stud had stayed closer to his grandmother than the rest of his stuffy family. Her noise drew a lot of attention, and I could see Abigail, Danforth, and Vanessa approaching out of the corner of my eye.

"Are you well, Mother Franklin?" Abigail asked in a singsong voice, looking at everyone around the area, clearly hoping no one was paying attention to the cackling woman.

"Yes, I'm fine. Don't hover!" she snapped at the Southern queen. "Eva was just telling me about her schooling and such. You know she designs clothes? That dress is one of her originals. Beautiful work. Nice to see a woman with some talent dating my Bo-Bo. Just look at this lap quilt! Handmade original!"

Abigail stuttered, "Ah—well—it is very nice."

Vanessa looked a little sick.

Danforth gulped down his glass of that hideous wine and

reached out to a passing waiter for another.

I tried not to laugh at the name Bo-Bo but lost the battle.

"What's so funny?" Abigail all but hissed at me. I felt Stud's fingers tighten on my shoulders, but I raised my hand to rest on his. Bea caught the calming gesture and nodded her approval.

"I'm just imagining what the other club members will say the first time I call him 'Little Bo-Bo.' I've got some serious firepower now! Thanks, Mrs. Franklin!"

"Oh, call me Nana. I ain't been Mrs. Franklin for years."

I lightly stroked my fingers over Stud's and felt him relax again. I really was having a pretty good time, considering. Just a few hours more until the party was over. I could survive this.

"Aren't you getting tired, Mother Franklin? Bea, maybe it's time Mother Franklin retires for the night," Abigail dismissively asserted. I began to wonder again whose party was this really supposed to be?

"I'm enjoying my grandson, whom I haven't seen in way too many years, and you lot aren't going to stop me!" She turned her gaze to Stud. "You bring your motorbike, boy?"

Stud answered with a big grin breaking out over his face. "Yes, ma'am, I did. You think you're up for it?"

"Abso-fucking-lutely!" The old woman chortled, much to the continued embarrassment of Abigail. "Best birthday present ever is to ride bitch with my grandson!"

Abigail turned bright red. Vanessa froze like a marble statue.

Danforth grabbed another glass. Stud laughed loudly, and I lost it completely.

"You go, Nana!" I shouted and wiped at the tears coming from my eyes. "I hope when I reach ninety, I can still ride bitch. No, scratch that. I'm getting my own bike. I hope I can still ride it at ninety!"

The old woman held up her hand for a high-five, which I tapped. "You go, girlfriend!"

Bea had put away her yarn in a big colorful bag next to her chair. "Guess I'll get the cane and help you out to the driveway. Beau, you get your bike and meet us there. Thelma, you do what Beau says and he'll keep you safe."

Stud leaned down and whispered in my ear. "Are you okay on your own for a bit?"

I reached up and caressed his cheek. "I'm good, babe. I'll wander around a bit until you get back. Go take your grandma for a ride."

CHAPTER SIXTEEN

He pressed his lips to my temple and left them there a long time. One last shoulder squeeze and he was gone, leaving me with his mother and brother. Vanessa murmured something about the restroom and made her escape. Danforth frowned hugely at the retreating back of his wife and downed the rest of his glass in one long gulp before reaching for another. Someone was well on his way to getting wasted tonight.

Abigail sniffed and drew herself up into ramrod straightness. "I don't know what your game is by being here with Beauregard, but I will assure you, Eva, you do not belong."

Wow! Talk about being blunt.

"You don't have to tell me that, Abby." She stiffened further, if that was even possible. "No games, though. What you see is what you get. It seems Stud doesn't think he belongs here either. Why else would he leave it all behind?"

"He has his trust still, so he didn't leave it all," she spat. "He's just out sowing oats or something. He'll come back. He has to."

I stood up, towering over the indignant woman with a huge stick up her ass. Nope, not a stick. A fucking two-by-four! "You have no idea who your son really is, do you?" I walked off, leaving her to hiss and spit in outrage, but managed to tune her out.

I needed the restroom myself and went into the one on the shining pool deck rather than take a chance on running into Vanessa on the way to the house. There were three unoccupied stalls and I was grateful for a moment of privacy. Hiding in a bathroom stall was not my intention, but when another couple of women came in, that's just what I did.

"*I can't believe Beau actually showed his face tonight! Poor Vannie!*"

"*He should be ashamed of himself after leaving her like he did! And joining up with that motorcycle gang? Vannie was so humiliated!*"

Wait, what? Stud and Vanessa were a thing?

"*She did okay marrying Danny, though. Terrible they can't have children.*"

"*Oh I know. They've been trying for years! I hear Abigail has been calling Beau for a while now, trying to get him to come back in the family*" fold. She and her husband are desperate to get him wedded and bedded so he can get the next generation of Franklins going. You know, to ensure the family businesses."

"Hmm—I certainly wouldn't mind that part! The bedding, I mean. That man can melt ice cubes in winter, he is so hot!"

"Not if I get him first! He's got his own trust from his grandparents, so he doesn't need his daddy's money. Danny went through his grandfather's inheritance already on that waste of a vineyard. Worst wine I've ever had!"

"Oh, yes indeed."

I couldn't decide if the rest of their sticky sweet Southern-accented conversation was hilarious, stupid, or insulting. Probably a combination of all three.

"What about that woman he brought with him? Who is that?"

"I know! She's so big and butch looking. Looks like one of the trainers at my gym!"

"I heard she works at a construction company. You know? The kind that builds stuff?"

I slapped my hand over my mouth to stifle my laughter. What other kind of construction was there?

"No refinement at all! Dresses real nice though."

"Beau Sr. will never allow her in the family. Abigail would just have a fit!"

"Ooh, but wouldn't that be a sight to watch!"

Both women finally exited, and I was able to get out myself. I looked around at the crowd, eating and drinking. Artificial party, artificial plants, artificial people. What a fucking soap opera! I was right. Maybe at one time Beau belonged here, but Stud definitely did not. The sooner we could get away, the better.

I wandered through the garden, mostly to get away from the crowd. These weren't my people and never would be. The flowers and plants looked even more fake in the hanging lights. The noise faded as I went deeper into the garden and found myself in the inner maze. The lights weren't as bright here and I was able to feel a better sense of solitude, which I sorely needed.

As I made my way back to the party, I heard noises coming from near the gazebo and stayed hidden behind a wall of thick bushes as I approached. I didn't know what I expected but the sight that met my eyes was not it.

Vanessa was bent over a stone bench, her short skirt hiked up around her hips and panties down around her ankles. She was getting the bejeezus fucked out of her, but not by her husband. Beau Sr. stood behind her, pants open, pumping in and out of her, grunting with every thrust, banging into her harder and harder.

What the fuck?

"Nice to see them keep it in the family, right?" a drunken voice slurred in my ear. I jumped but managed not to scream. Danforth was leaning against a tall stone statue and apparently had been for some time, watching his wife getting drilled by his father.

"Daddy dearest has good taste, eh? My fuckin' wife," he muttered as he drank from a bottle held loosely in one hand. I could see he had given up on using a glass. "Goddamn bitch."

I was sure none of the fancy etiquette books in the library had any advice on how to handle this!

"I'm—uh—sorry?" I responded in a low voice, wishing I'd never left the party. I could hear the sounds filtering through the small maze. Pretty bold to be going at it with your daughter-in-law that close to a public gathering!

"Yeah, well, it's my fault," Danforth slurred. "Ayin't got the ballz to stan' up to daddy dearest. Beau got 'em all. My fuckin' brother! He left us. Got out! I haddoo take on hiz shit! Hiz fuckin' sloppy seconds! Or should I say sloppy thirdz?"

The sounds of slapping flesh and low grunts got louder as they reached their climax. Or at least one of them was. It was hard not to watch, but I managed to turn away.

He swallowed the last of the bottle and put a hand to his forehead. "She's fucked-up inside. His fuckin' fault. Goddamn bastard."

"I'm—uh—going to go now." Awkward didn't even begin to describe this situation.

"Why d'you wanna do that?" Danforth dropped the bottle. He moved toward me and I pressed against the prickly bushes, trying to keep him out of my personal space. "Show'z jus' gettin' started. He'll do her up the ass before he'z finished. My fuckin' wife."

This was not something I wanted to see or even know about. Jesus! How much had he had to drink tonight? He stank worse than any of my brothers on a bender. I was done.

"This is some sick shit! I don't blame Stud for escaping this crazy-ass family! I'm leaving," I said firmly, attempting to move out of his way.

His hands came up to grip my shoulders tightly and pull me into his body. He was stronger than he looked, and I was taken by surprise. He ran his wet mouth over my neck, leaving a sloppy trail behind. My stomach lurched at the slimy feel.

"Get off me!" I hissed, pushing at him, trying to escape both him and the bushes behind me that were scratching into my back and arms.

He roughly grabbed a breast, squeezing it painfully. "You suck cock? Mah wifey does. I seen 'er."

He forced a hand between my legs and gripped me hard.

To hell with this!

I shoved the drunk man hard and screamed as loud as I could. "GET THE FUCK OFF ME YOU FUCKING SICK BASTARD!" He landed against the stone statue hard enough to knock it over. It crashed through the bushes, exposing Beau Sr. and Vanessa, still at it. The noise was deafening.

I vaguely heard a squeal and a shuffle coming from the direction of the gazebo, and the sound of running feet coming towards us. Danforth wasn't done. He came at me again in a red-faced rage, pulling back a fist to take a swing at my head.

Fuck my life! Not again! was my first thought as my own fist leapt up to crack across his face, sending an arc of blood spraying from his nose. My second thought was to duck under his flailing arm and come up with a hard punch to his middle. He "oofed" and bent over, all the wine he had consumed rushing out of his mouth and splashing on the broken stones. Ugh! My shoes got some of it too. Molly would be pissed. That was the absolute last straw!

"What the fuck is *wrong* with you people?" I yelled, my Irish bitch in full form. "I've never seen so much fucked-up shit in my life! Why in the fuck would Stud ever come back to this crap? Is *this* what it means to be rich? It's one big stinking pile of bullshit!"

By that time, more spectators had arrived, mouths open and aghast at the sight of Danforth on his knees, puking his guts out. Just beyond us, Beau Sr. and Vanessa were struggling to get their clothes back in order. I caught Vanessa tripping over her panties as she jerked at her tight skirt, trying to get it over her hips and her ass covered. Her face was beet red, the first real color I'd seen her wear.

"What's going on here?" Abigail's voice rang out. She pushed through the crowd and stopped short. I saw her eyes widen as she looked at her son, still curled up and heaving on the ground. They narrowed again, this time at me. "You piece of trash! What did you do?"

She strode forward, all indignant, ready to tear me a new one. When she spotted Vanessa and her husband, she stopped short again, her mouth opening and closing like a fish.

"Beau? What are you doing?" she asked, all the fight gone out of her.

Beau Sr. was tucking himself away and zipping up his pants. Vanessa was pulling up her panties and looking everywhere but at her mother-in-law.

"Again? And in public? How could you?" she wailed.

I wasn't sure if her question was directed at her or him.

"It's not what you think, Abigail," Beau Sr. started. "This isn't a big deal."

"Nor is it the first time." Stud's deep voice rang out. He strode through the crowd past his mom and straight up to his dad. "You were fucking her when she was engaged to me. I saw you in your home office the night I left. My fiancée bent over and my father ramming it in. Looks like nothin's changed."

I'd never heard this amount of pure rage from anyone before. It was deadly. I could feel the force of it radiating from every pore in his body. My Irish bitch got subdued and quiet. I'd process the engagement news later.

Vanessa found her voice. "It's not... I'm... I had to. I loved you! Love you even now so much, but I had to do it!"

"No you didn't," Stud replied, deadly cold.

"Beau, please understand!" she pleaded. "We—my parents—we were broke and—and—"

"Don't you think I knew that? Don't you think I would've helped your parents? Used my trust to save that abysmal vineyard of yours? I was ready to lay the world at your feet, but it wasn't good enough because we wouldn't be able to live rich. You would've had to give up your expensive tea parties, club lunches, and shit like that for a while, but I was working my ass off, trying to give you everything you wanted. I thought we were in that together. Then I found out you were *fucking my goddamn father!*"

Oh, this was bad. Gasps and exclamations rippled through the crowd as the dirtiest of the family laundry was thrown to the ground.

"You're a user, Vannie. He needed an old family name for the connections. Your people only had the name left and needed his money. Marriage to me was the final prize. Perfect fairy-tale story to show the world, perfect cesspool hidden underneath. Only no one counted on you getting pregnant, did they?"

Holy shit!

"The child was aborted because you didn't know if he was my son or my father's."

Oh. My. Ever. Loving. God.

The silence. Utter silence from every person there. Abigail was white as a sheet. Vanessa was reeling back and grasping at the stiff Beau Sr. He ignored her.

Danforth finally stood up and staggered over to Stud.

"Fuck you, *brother!*" he spat out and tried to tackle Stud. He didn't even have to lift a finger, just move back and Danforth was on the ground again, sniveling and vomiting more.

Beau Sr. puffed himself up and shook off Vanessa's grasping hands. "Beauregard Franklin Jr., you are no longer welcome in this house. You've brought nothing but shame and strife, and I will never again claim you as my son," he declared, as if he had been the one wronged.

I wanted so bad to laugh. *That's all you got, old man? A plastic house with plastic plants? Plastic wife so into appearances she alienated her own son? Plastic pussy so into her own self she couldn't see the value that was right in front of her? Plastic younger son so weak in character he couldn't stand up to you and keep his wife from fucking around? If this was living rich, someone else could have it! I'd rather live with less, than be living as less.*

I stayed silent, though. This was Stud's fight. I was backup.

"No problem there. I left a long time ago. Remember?" Stud turned his blue eyes to me, glancing at the bruises on my arms. I held up my equally bruised knuckles to show him he didn't need to defend me. I'd already taken care of that business.

"Get your stuff together and meet me out front. We're not staying," he ordered darkly.

"What about your stuff?" I asked.

"Just get my cut for me. The rest can stay and rot." He strode off, the crowd parting like the Red Sea for him.

I quickly changed and stuffed everything into my pack. I managed to stuff most of his things into his pack as well. I grabbed his cut, knowing he would want to put it on his back as soon as he could. He took it from me and all but sighed in relief when he slid it around his shoulders. That connection with the club was more real than anything else in his life. He stowed the packs and handed me my helmet.

He grabbed my wrist before I strapped it on.

"I can't stay here tonight. You already know that, but I'm not ready to go back to Bryson City, and I'm not ready to take you back to your family. Will you go somewhere and stay with me? Just for a day or two?"

I hadn't hesitated to take his back for this disastrous visit, and I wouldn't let him down now. I wasn't ready to go back to my family just yet either. I could feel his need and that was more important than a new job site.

"Let's go," I confirmed, lifting the helmet over my head.

"Do you care where?" he asked, his voice muffled.

"Nope. I trust you."

We mounted in silence and I wrapped myself around him, hugging him close, hoping he felt my support.

He revved the engine and drove off, leaving his childhood behind for the second and final time.

CHAPTER SEVENTEEN

I woke up to the watery smell and sound of a well-used air conditioner. The thing rattled and wheezed, but did put out a cool mineral-scented breeze. We would need it while we were here.

We'd driven for several hours, and I spent much of it dozing at Stud's back. It's a wonder I didn't fall off. He headed east and seemed to know where he was going, so I just hung on for the ride. Sometime before dawn, we arrived at a seventies style motel that had a vacancy sign flashing. The kind that has individual rooms in one long row in an L shape. The owners had their own house/ quarters at one end and were always on duty. We were checked in by a short gray-haired older woman in a flowery red zip-up robe. She sleepily answered our ring, swiped Stud's card, and handed us a real key complete with a diamond-shaped tag stating we were in room seven. He only got one room for both of us, but at that point, I just didn't care.

I stretched, feeling my muscles protest at the movement. Don't let anyone ever tell you riding a motorcycle is easy! If I was this sore from sitting behind Stud, I could only imagine how he was feeling.

A band tightened around my middle, pulling me back as I shifted. I found myself glancing down at Stud's arm encircling me, his warm hand on my stomach, holding me in place. My bare stomach. I wasn't wearing pants. Just a tank top and my lacy panties from last night.

Holy shit!

I froze in place. It hadn't occurred to me when I tumbled into the bed so much earlier that we would be sleeping in it together. He was spooning close to my back and I could feel the heat of his body against me. His thumb began lazily stroking my skin, just under my breast. My heart rate picked up at the light touch. Only an inch or so more and that digit would be stroking my tightening nipple. He huffed a bit and moved closer, pressing his hips into my backside. He wasn't exactly awake, but he was definitely up. I could feel the outline of his morning wood grinding behind me. I supposed this should have pissed me off, but I found myself wishing that stroking thumb would move up those few inches.

Instead, he kissed and nipped at the spot where my shoulder and neck met. His teeth sent a jolt down my spine, and it was all I could do not to yelp and contract like a turtle.

"Morning, Cactus," he rumbled as he shifted and got out of the bed. "Room has one of those coffee maker things, but the coffee is usually shit. I'm gonna go get some real coffee and bagels or something. Be back in a bit."

I watched him move into the tiny bathroom, his tight ass covered by black boxer briefs. How can a mouth both water and go dry at the same time? I'd swear mine did just that.

The sounds of him using the toilet and switching on the shower filtered into the room. I scrambled out of the bed myself and leaned over the small cramped dresser to look at myself in the mirror hanging above it on the plain beige wall. Red-ringed eyes smeared with leftover mascara floated in a sea of tangled red hair. I licked my fingers and tried to wipe away some of the black. It didn't help. I'd just fished out my hairbrush from my pack when I heard the shower go off. Shit! I was still only in a tank and my panties. I was rummaging through my pack again to find the clean pair of jeans I brought when Stud's arms came around me and pulled me against his hot, wet body.

"Be back in a bit, babe." He gave me a squeeze and kissed me on the temple. I raised a hand and ran my fingers over his stubble and murmured something affirmative.

While he was gone, I texted Connor to let him know something had come up and I wasn't sure when I would be arriving at the job site. Then I showered with the motel's version of soap but my own shampoo and conditioner. Dressing was easy as I didn't have a lot of choices, but I did have fresh underwear, which led me to wonder how long we would be here—wherever here was.

I got my answer soon enough as I heard a knock on the door and opened it to Stud holding a carrier with two large paper cups and a white bag.

"Oh yes! You just became my favorite biker of all time!" I overenthused and took the carrier from his hand.

"I've always been your favorite biker of all time," he answered, his half smile lighting up on his face.

I rolled my eyes. "Not unless you brought Danishes as well," I quipped back.

He opened the bag and with a flourish and produced a sticky cinnamon roll.

"Yum! I think just looking made my butt expand a bit!" I made a grab for the sweet confection.

Stud laughed. Finally a real laugh, like he was back at the club, having a good time, carrying on and joking around. I knew it wouldn't last, but for now, I had my man back.

My man. Could I really say that?

I found out where we were the moment we stepped outside of

the tiny motel room. A long flat beach greeted my eyes, along with calm waves rippling in the blazing sun. I could see a bank of clouds on the horizon indicating a storm was approaching, but it would be much later before it arrived.

"So where are we?" I asked, turning to Stud as he took my hand and we headed for the sandy expanse.

"Beach," he said.

I slugged him in the shoulder. "I knew that part, smartass. What beach?"

He rubbed the spot where I hit him. "Damn, Cactus! Such violence!" he teased.

He was covering. I knew it and he knew it, but he wasn't ready to say or do anything yet. I hoped he would be soon.

"North Carolina Outer Banks, 'bout halfway between Rodanthe and Waves. I picked up some flip-flops at the beach store where I got the coffees. The sand is too hot for barefoot walking."

He was right. I could feel the heat burning through the thin layer of foam. We walked hand in hand, making comments on the houses, watching kids run and play in the surf, skirting around half-built sand castles, and nodding at families who had set up giant umbrellas for the day.

"It's a great place. Peaceful. A lot of areas still untouched or protected and kept natural. A lot of history. Some amazing things happened up and down these islands. Blackbeard the pirate, the

Wright Brothers making the first successful airplane, the lost colony. It's an amazing place. It became one of my favorites."

Stud rambled as we walked, telling me more about the islands' history. We spent the day riding to the different sights. Climbing the Hatteras Lighthouse, going through the Graveyard of the Atlantic Museum, riding the ferry to Ocracoke Island, and seeing that beautiful white lighthouse as well. The whole time we roamed and meandered the islands, he either held my hand or kept his arm around my shoulders or waist. He wasn't smothering me, but just seemed to want me close at all times.

I still didn't know how long we would stay there and I hoped Stud would tell me soon. I was sure Connor had blown up my phone with texts, but I had turned it off earlier. We pulled into a small restaurant with an outdoor seating area with a good view of the Pamlico Sound. The smell of boiling seafood floated on the air. We got a table outside and ordered the house special. A steaming bucket of fresh-caught shrimp, soft shell crab, and oysters was placed in front of us as well as a platter of fried trout and Spanish mackerel. I thought I was going to burst before we got up from the table.

"How 'bout some ice cream?" Stud asked, sticking a toothpick between his teeth as we left. I tried to pay for some of the stuff we did during the day, but every time I pulled out my wallet, he growled at me and swiped his card.

"You've got to be kidding?" I joked, leaning into him. "It will take me a week to burn off the load we just put away."

"I could stay here a week," he said, a serious tone in his voice. "Maybe longer. It was here I finally broke away from my family and found myself."

We were walking on the pier, our shoes making hollow sounds. A lone fisherman was packing up for the day, as the twilight was coming in as well as the threatening storm clouds. It had been a good day. A good day for both of us. We reached the end of the pier and I breathed in the salty tang. Stud looked out over the water but didn't seem to see it. He gripped the weather-worn railing and started speaking.

"You have eyes and ears, so you know I don't get along very well with my family. I don't even really think of them much, now. The only person left in that house I want to see more often is my grandmother, but that's pretty limited since I'd have to see them too. I think sometimes if I never laid eyes on them again I could be content for the rest of my life."

He took a breath and fisted his hands as he so often did when he was trying to hold back and stay in control.

"When I was a kid, I was expected to be the best. Top grades, top athlete, class president, playing double bass in the orchestra, didn't matter what it was. No exceptions. No praise if I succeeded, but damn if I didn't get the shit beat out of me if I failed. I'm not talking about physical beatings. Dear old dad would never stoop to spanking his children, but I swear, my father can draw blood using his words. Once, I brought home four first-place trophies and one second place from a track and field competition. My mother never attended any meets, but my father came once in a while—and he came to that one. Not one word about all the first places. Only the second place. Two tenths of a second difference was all it took for my father to tell me I was a loser and would never amount to much. The other trophies meant nothing unless I won them all. I even won the overall first place for the day. Still wasn't good enough. I was in seventh grade when that happened."

He paused as if in some memory. I placed a hand on his shoulder, rubbing up and down, but staying silent. This was his time.

"My mother wasn't any better. Sometimes I wonder how she and my father managed to produce two children. Dan and I were raised by an army of nannies and sitters. Abigail was too busy with her charity boards and club lunches to be bothered with us. We were too messy to be around, apparently. Calling her 'mom' was more like an insult to her than the title of pride it should have been. Dan and I were not close growing up. You'd think we would be, but our father used to make fun of him a lot. Telling him he would never be as good as me. Hearing that shit for years can really take a toll on a kid. The nannies never stayed around long. My father ended up fucking most of them, and Abigail would fire them when she found out. I remember catching him a few times. He always liked to take them from behind. Apparently he still does."

My heart hurt. Stud may have had more given to him growing up, but that didn't mean he had what really counted.

"Nana was my only escape. I spent as much time as I could with her, outside of tutors, lessons, sports, and whatever else I had to do. She was the most real person I knew and the only one to love me for me. Not the shiny awards or the continuation of the family bloodline. I got into Duke on academic merit. Do you have any idea how hard that is? My father said I was an embarrassment because I didn't make the basketball team. Funny thing is, Nana hated Duke and was a big NC State fan until I got in. She put on a Duke sweatshirt and promptly became their biggest fan. My father raged at me for hours over the basketball team. Abigail wasn't even interested.

"I was in law school when I met Vanessa. She came from an old family name, old family money. Abigail and Beau were thrilled at the connections. I guess it helped I fell in love with her. Hook, line, and sinker. Asked her to marry me just after I graduated and started at the family firm. Put a big rock on her finger, planned the big wedding, looked at big houses. That's what I was supposed to do, right? Fairy-tale stuff. I thought life was going to be good and I could get out from under my father's thumb. I shared with her my dreams and that my plans were to build a name for myself, and in a few years, break from my father's firm to open my own office, my own place, be my own man. I thought she was behind me with this."

He gave a short, bitter laugh. "Couple months before the wedding, I was working nearly round the clock, spending hours at the office, working case after case to earn my place there and get the money I needed to go out on my own. I forgot some important papers one afternoon and came home to get them. I found my father in the home office with her, fucking like animals. I can still remember her yelling out 'fuck me harder, Daddy' just before she saw me in the doorway. He didn't stop, he just let me watch while he finished. His only words to me were 'don't be late for dinner' when he left the room. She didn't say anything. Just stood there and wouldn't even meet my eyes."

I probably looked like a bug as big as my eyes got but I managed to keep quiet and let him finish. Daytime soap operas weren't this bad in the drama department.

He took a big breath.

"I left that night. Left my suits, ties, all the trappings of that life, just left it all. I came here to the banks for a few days. I thought I would just get away for a bit. Get my head together and figure out my next move. While I was here, I got a call from the women's clinic telling me Vanessa was going to be kept overnight for observation. Apparently, she listed me as the first emergency contact. She had been getting sick a lot. Claimed it was the flu and she would be over it before the big wedding day. I was so naïve back then or maybe so involved in work, I didn't question anything she said. Turns out it wasn't flu. She was pregnant."

He closed his eyes and dropped his head as if the weight was too much.

"They said the abortion had done some damage, but she was fine and resting, and I could come pick her up the next day. It was all very hush-hush, very discreet, no one outside the family knew. I don't think even I was supposed to know about it except for that phone call."

Holy shit! I thought. I pulled at his rigid arms and pushed myself into his body, wrapping around him as far as I could reach. He clung to me.

"Fuck, Eva. I didn't really care if there was a chance the baby was my brother. I was ready to love my son or daughter no matter what, and that was taken away from me before I even knew I was a father. I cannot forgive that, ever."

I could feel his body tremble as the emotional tide in him rose.

"I sold my car here at the banks and bought my first motorcycle and spent some time learning to ride. I'd always wanted one, but Beau had forbidden it and Abigail always called it 'unrefined' or 'gauche.' They no longer had a say about anything in my life and I didn't want to own anything that reminded me of it. I just rode. Up and down the coast. Georgia. Florida. Staying wherever I stopped. I didn't have to worry about money. Dear old dad couldn't take away my trust. I just roamed. I was shattered. No purpose. No life. I finally roamed west and found myself in the mountains. Found the Dragon Runners. They put me back together. I owe them my life."

I felt tears pricking at my eyes. I pressed my cheek firmer into his shoulder, squeezing hard. These heart-to-heart talks were not very familiar to me as the only ones I ever had with any depth were the occasional ones with Connor. I wanted to help Stud, but I really didn't know what to say. I just held on, hard as oak, and hoped he got something out of it.

"I'm still fucked-up, though. Deep down inside, I'm still so goddamn fucked-up. I'm half a man, living a half-life. I can hide it really well thanks to my childhood training, but I'm so goddamn broken, I don't think I'll ever truly be whole again."

I could hear his voice wavering as he clutched at me. He was about to lose it and lose it big. This, I could do something about.

"Bullshit," I announced to his shoulder.

He jumped at my harsh announcement.

"What?" he asked, startled.

"You heard me. I call bullshit," I said again, pulling away to look in his face. His eyes were red and a look of confusion shone bright in them.

"You know me, Stud. You know I'm not going to sugarcoat things all pretty, pat you on the head, say 'there, there, dear' and tell you some bullshit story. You had a childhood that sucks monkey butt. A big-ass monkey butt at that! Your dad is an ass, your mom is a snob, your brother is weak, and your ex is a fucking coward. All of that was a big challenge for you. Bigger than a lotta men can take on, but you dealt with it and moved on. Listen to me good here, Stud. You're not broken. You're not fucked up. You got dealt a heavy blow. A fucking big one that would knock the knees from under anyone with a heart, but you're still here and you got away from it. You survived and moved on. You found a life and a damn good one. There's no reason for you to think those assholes get a say in anything. They do not own you! They do not define you!"

I took a breath, just getting wound up. This was the best way I knew to deal with my brothers. Meet them head-on in any type of conflict. Stud, however, didn't argue back, get mad, blow up, or have any of the other reactions I expected.

He seized my hair in a firm grip, pulled my head back, and slammed his mouth down on mine. He took over, kissing me hard, wild, and wet. I answered back just as hard, my body getting hot and my mind focusing on him and only him. The pounding beat of his heart, the feel of his hands, and the taste of his mouth all consumed my awareness.

Somehow we ended up back in the motel room. I didn't know how we got there. I just knew my whole body was on fire, a heat I was determined to quench. Stud yanked my shirt over my head just inside the door and jerked down my bra strap, peeling away the cup and baring me to him. I cried out when he sucked my nipple into his mouth, electricity zapping straight between my legs. I clawed at his shirt until I got it over his head and we tumbled onto the bed, him pulling awkwardly at my jeans and panties until he got them off me. He pulled my legs apart and was right there, licking and sucking my clit. I arched my back, grabbing a handful of his hair as the blaze consumed me.

I wasn't stupid or naïve about sex. I may not have been experienced, but I knew a thing or two from watching movies and seeing the porn my brothers tried to keep hidden from me. Nothing had prepared me for what it was like, having Stud do what he was doing to me. I writhed under his mouth, grinding at the intense sensation, like a bowstring drawn too tight. He pushed a finger into my untried channel and the slide of that hard digit was more than I could take. I screamed, losing complete control as I experienced the wildest climax I'd ever imagined was possible.

The fire was banked for the moment. Stud licked above my oversensitive flesh a few times before rising up to meet my stunned eyes. If this is how sex felt, I wanted more!

"You taste so good, baby." His voice rumbled as he settled himself over me, his elbows to either side of my shoulders. He lowered his mouth to mine, and I sampled my own flavor. His dick was rock hard and I could feel it through his jeans as he pressed against me, but he made no move to go any further. I could feel the tension in his body as he hesitated, and my own frustration mounted.

My voice came out breathless. "I'm ready, Stud. Please!"

He raised his head to meet my eyes again. He stroked a hand through my hair, trailing over my cheek and neck. "I really want to be the one to take your virginity, baby, but I don't know that I ought to have that honor, and especially when I don't know where this will lead. I want to explore a future with you, but I'm taking you back to your family tomorrow and then heading back to Bryson City. We haven't really talked about us, and you deserve more than a one-night stand from me or anyone else. Maybe after the Wilmington job—"

I growled as I grabbed his shoulders and flipped him. He uttered a single "oomph" when he landed on his back. I popped the buttons on the fly of his jeans and jerked the fabric down as far as I could. I got on top of him and seized my prize. How could he be so hard with skin so soft? Stroking him was like touching velvet-covered iron. A thick bead of precum appeared at the slit, and I smeared it over the head. He closed his eyes, and I heard him groan.

"You aren't *taking* anything, Stud. I'm *giving* it to you! I've waited a long time for someone I wanted and cared about for this, and I choose you. If we're meant to have a future after the Wilmington job, we'll figure it out. You're my best friend, my shoulder support, my listener... I love you! There, I said it. I love you!"

I positioned him at my entrance and moved down, working the head inside my body. It hurt like a mother, but pain wasn't something I'd ever been afraid of. I'd had enough injuries in my life to know what real pain was like.

"Oh Christ, Eva! Slow down, baby."

"I don't want to." I slid down even further, taking more of him in my body. The burn was getting more intense and I gasped, not knowing what to do but not wanting to stop either.

"Hang on, baby. Let me help." His hands grabbed my hips and guided my frantic movements. He rocked into me back and forth a few times and with one long thrust, he broke through and filled me. *Fuck, that hurt!*

He stayed still, letting me get used to him being a part of me. The discomfort faded as I straddled his hips, feeling the sensation of tightness, fullness, and rightness of belonging. This wasn't as much pain as it was passage into something deeper. We fit together like perfect puzzle pieces. I shifted on top of him, not sure what to do next, but wanted to move, wanted to feel that hard push in my body again, wanted something more.

He shifted underneath me and steered me with his hands still at my hips. I felt him press against a spot as he rolled and ground inside me. The fire in my belly rekindled and it wasn't long before I moved with him. I threw back my head and leaned back, meeting each upward thrust with a downward one of my own. My whole world was concentrated on the man below me, his hard flesh melding into mine, and the burn between my legs. He slipped his hand over my stomach and between my legs, his thumb circling my slippery clit. Another climax hit me like a freight train, and I screamed with the intensity of it. Stud flipped me to my back and took control, pumping into me harder and faster. He shouted and jerked out of me at the last moment, coming all over my stomach, hot juice coating me as he finished himself off with a few strokes of his hand.

We lay there, side by side, for several long minutes, just breathing and touching, heat pouring from our sweaty skin. He finally got up, kissed me lightly, and went into the bathroom. I heard the sink run and a moment later he was back, sitting on the bed and wiping the sticky residue from my stomach with a warm, wet towel. He slid the cloth between my legs and cleaned me there too.

"Are you okay? Did I hurt you?" he asked while he traced the hard slabs of my stomach muscles, his fingers outlining the delineations.

"No, I'm not hurt," I said. I didn't know what I was. Definitely sore, but I felt like I was glowing, satisfied, fulfilled, incredible, and more than anything thing else, pure and total happiness. I'm a happy person in general, at least I always thought I was happy, but this feeling was a height I'd never experienced before. I didn't think it possible. I came down a bit, thinking this may be the only time I had it.

"I'm great, in fact." I smiled and placed my fingers over Stud's bicep as he leaned over me. "That was—I don't have the right words. Fantastic, I guess I can say, but it was a lot more than that."

His eyes watched his fingers as they continued to reverently stroke over my stomach and thighs. "It was more for me too."

I stayed on my back while he kept caressing my body, smoothing his hand up and down. I did the same, running my fingers over his arms, tracing the details of the tattoos on his shoulders. The place between my legs throbbed and ached a bit, but it felt good. Maybe all the hard, physical conditioning I'd had all my life had something to do with that.

His fingers brushed over my breasts and my nipples tightened up, sending little pulses through my stomach. He leaned over and took one in his mouth, suckling it gently while stroking the other with his thumb. Twin sensations ran down my body and settled between my legs. My eyes closed, and I relaxed further, letting myself simply enjoy.

"I didn't wear a condom. That's why I didn't come inside you. This is the first time in years I've gone without, but just so you know, I'm tested and safe," he stated against my breast. "I have a few wrappers with me, but I don't want to fuck you again."

My heart stopped at his sentence, and my eyes flew open as a stab of real hurt hit me in the chest.

"If you're not too sore, I really want to make love to you. This time slow and easy so I can watch you come and make it safe so I can come inside you."

My heart started beating again, faster.

His dick was hardening again. I could see it rise from where it rested on his thigh. I reached for it, running my fingers down its length and circling it with my hand. He inhaled sharply and got even harder.

We made love like he said. Slow, easy, him playing with me like the master of lovemaking he was reputed to be. He drew it out until I was a bundle of need, and when I climaxed, it was long and deep with him staring into my eyes, watching me with an intensity that made the moment even more intimate. He stayed inside me, and when he reached his own height, he groaned and collapsed on top of me, holding me tight, buried deep in me, and I felt each pulse as he came. He whispered in my ear, so lightly I might have missed it, "Love you too, Eva."

CHAPTER EIGHTEEN

Stud woke first the next morning and watched Eva sleep for a few minutes. She was on her side, one hand curled under the cheap motel pillow and the other palm up in front of her body. She was peaceful, breathing deep and even. Stud felt a satisfaction he hadn't felt in a long time. A contentment that life was good and would only get better. The feeling became bittersweet, as today he was taking her back to her family. He knew she should be happy getting back to them, getting back to work, getting back to her life, but there was a sadness in her as well. He hoped she wouldn't regret the time they'd spent together. Last night they'd made love as many times as he had condoms, three total. She never refused when he reached for her, and every time was beautiful. Even if it was the only night he ever had with her, he would remember and cherish every moment. These last few days had meant so much to him, and the precious gift she gave him he would treasure for a lifetime.

He checked out and took them both to a greasy spoon diner for breakfast before getting on the road. Stud put on his best face, smiling and teasing Eva, trying his best to act as if it were business as usual, but inside he was breaking. He watched as she turned her phone back on as they were mounting up to make the long ride to Wilmington. It dinged with several missed texts. One was from Connor sending her the address of the RV and her tiny house. The worksite was downtown and had no place to park those two vehicles. The other was from Psalm asking if she had more stuff to sell. All of the lounge pants had sold at the festival and most of the lap quilts. People were asking for more and some wanted to commission bigger quilts. Stud smiled and hugged her as she bounced around showing her excitement.

"Knew it would happen, Cactus," Stud said as he messed with the bike. He was genuinely happy for her. "Just remember the little folks when you become famous." He stood back and bowed with a flourish, presenting the extra cushion he installed on the bike for her to sit. He laughed and winced, rubbing his shoulder when she punched him. She scowled at his play but did thank him for his thoughtfulness.

Stud made sure they took a few breaks as they rode, partially to give her a break and partially to draw out the time. *It's not like I'll never see her again,* he reasoned with himself. She had to come back to Bryson City and get the rest of her stuff. She still had the sewing machine and a few clothes left in his room. Besides, she wanted to be at the wedding. She had to finish the wedding dress for Kat. Stud had heard all about how Molly had wanted a bunch of sparkle, sequins, beads and stuff, but Kat managed to calm her down and got the dress that was more to her taste. Kat had seemed to be pleased with the results. Maybe custom dresses could be another item in Psalm's shop.

Stud kept giving himself silent pep talk after silent pep talk, the constant voice in his head ranging from *it will be okay, I'll see her again, this is not the end* to *I can't lose this, it will never be the same!* A chorus of what-ifs spun around and around in his mind. *What if she never comes back? What if she does and things are different? What if she finds someone else at her next site? What if? What if?* Every hour or so, he thought about turning the bike around and heading back to Bryson City. Taking her to his home and making love to her until she agreed to stay with him or was too damn tired to argue.

His biggest fear and worst thought came to him as they passed a sign that said Wilmington City Limits. *What if I never feel this way again?*

Stud could tell something was wrong as he drove slowly up the street where the GPS was leading them. The living vehicles were parked in an empty store lot near the site, but not at it. He could see flashing police lights, fire trucks, and firemen in hard hats teeming over the area. The waning sun made the whole scene surreal. A sour, burnt charcoal smell filled the air, pungent and raw. Fire, obviously. A big one. He felt Eva's hands claw at his waist where she was hanging on and heard her in the helmet radio gasp out, "*What the fuck?*"

Stud coasted the bike as close to the scene as he could and put a leg down to steady it. Eva leapt off and was ready to rush into the chaos. Stud grabbed her hand and kept her back. She swung at him and tried to pull away, but Stud ignored her and held on as his brain processed what he was seeing. Connor was in a tremendous fight with his father; both men were yelling and gesturing wildly. This was not the easy-going diplomatic man who had worked side by side with Eva. This was a man who was on the absolute edge.

"Connor! Holy shit, Connor!" Stud heard Eva shout as she scrabbled her fingers on the helmet strap. He didn't say a word when she dropped the expensive piece of equipment to the ground and ran toward her brother. She hadn't seen yet what he had.

Conner stopping yelling at his dad when he heard Eva cry out. Instead of being happy to see her, he jammed both hands through his thick hair to the back of his head and turned as if unable to face her. Stud pulled off his own helmet and let it drop next to Eva's. He stared and his mouth got hard at the sight just beyond Connor's still form. He rushed to catch up. This was not good. Not in any sense of the word.

Stud saw the moment when Eva recognized the blackened, wet pile of smoldering wood sitting not too far in front of her. She stopped just short of Connor and her da, arms at her side, standing as still as marble as she finally saw the heap that was once her tiny house. Her truck hadn't been spared either. It was nothing more than burnt rubble as well.

"What? Why?" Eva was stuttering, her face white as a sheet. Stud came up behind her and wrapped his arms around her. She melted into him like she couldn't hold herself up any longer. Connor took notice of Stud's position and frowned even more, if that was even possible.

"Is everyone okay?" she asked in a small, quavering voice.

Fergus harrumphed. "Yes. Yes, everyone is fine. They're all at the job site working." He turned to Eva and pointed a finger at her. "That's where you should be, ya *cailín leisciúil!*"

Stud felt Eva freeze at the harsh tone. He held on and waited, counting down in his head. *Three—two—one—*

But it wasn't Eva who exploded, it was Connor.

"*Cailín leisciúil?* Are you fucking mad! You call your only daughter lazy and good for nothing? Jesus, Mary, and Joseph, you're a piece of work, Da!"

He pointed at the still smoking hot mess that was once Eva's home.

"This is your fault, ya damn Irish bastard! You have not the least respect for any of us! You know she doesn't allow smoking in her house. I told you twice not to smoke those damn cigars of yours in there. I had to put one out that you left sitting on the table a few nights ago. *On the fucking table!*"

Fergus turned red in the face. "My cigars didn't start this! That table had the wrong kind of finish! Whole house was badly made. Bad wiring. I'm surprised it didn't go up in flames long ago."

Connor was not done. His voice got louder and louder. "You've screwed up orders again, got the wrong dates for delivery, over booked the whole operation until we're spread so thin, we'll be lucky to finish this one anywhere near on time! Now you're making excuses, blaming everyone else for your mistakes. You've treated us like fucking slaves for years, and I've put up with it for the sake of my brothers and sister, but this is the absolute last straw! *I. Am. Done!*"

Stud felt Eva jerk in his arms at her brother's declaration.

Fergus went off. "What do you mean, 'done'? You can't just be 'done'! This is a family business! Your brothers need you!"

"I can't do this anymore!" Connor ranted on. It seemed cathartic, like a boil that just got lanced and all the poisons were draining out. "I've been covering your ass for years. I stuck around because of family. You certainly didn't worry about your sons or your daughter. Not with me taking care of things. We roam like Irish gypsies, and I'm sick of it. I'm almost thirty-five. Too old to be living in an RV with five other men, brothers or not. I want a real home and to find a wife and kids of my own. I've given all I can give. It's time for them to grow up and go their own way. It's past time for me to go."

He turned to Eva. "I'm so, so sorry, *a stóirín*. This was not supposed to happen, and I tried. The Lord above knows I tried. I'll take care of the insurance. We have everything covered. You'll need to stay in the RV for a wee bit. Best I can do for now."

"No," Eva stated, her voice low and devoid of emotion. "I love you, *mo run*."

"No?" Fergus blustered, but no one paid attention to the old man.

"Please get me out of here, Stud," she whispered.

Stud looked up at Connor and lifted an eyebrow. Their eyes met, man to man. Words weren't necessary. Connor's mouth relaxed, and he gave one short nod. "Good. Take care of her."

Stud led Eva back to the bike. She didn't resist as he strapped on her helmet, and then she mounted up behind him. Her grip was looser, but she still managed to hold on. Stud drove the short distance to the town of Leland. It was dark as he pulled into a Holiday Inn Express. She was quiet the entire trip, and this had Stud very worried. He'd seen Eva happy and laughing, mad as hell, working hard and cussing, arguing with anyone and everyone, always standing up strong, more ready for a fight than anyone else he knew. This Eva was like a gutted shell. This wasn't his Eva at all.

He checked them into a room. Eva went in and sat on the bed, staring and still processing. Her eyes were glazed and dilated, and her hands were shaking. *She's in shock,* Stud thought, remembering the state he was in when his world shattered and he'd been in pieces. He imagined it was the same for her and his heart bled a little, knowing what she was going through.

"Come on, baby. Let's get you warmed up in the shower." He pulled at her icy hands and she stood up to follow him into the bathroom. He turned on the water, making it as hot as he thought she could stand. He stripped them both quickly and got her under the spray, letting the water soak through her hair and run down her back. She shivered once, and he enfolded her again in his arms, pressing her breasts against his chest and wrapping her tight.

"You're safe, baby. I got you," he murmured, his lips to her wet head.

It was then that she broke. She cried out, her scream echoing in the tiled chamber. She clawed at him, fighting and gouging her fingers into his arms, chest, back, anywhere she could reach. She punched and hammered at him, twisting to get away, then clutched him close. Stud held on while she fought her way through. This took a long time, as she was a strong woman, physically and mentally. Stud knew he would be sporting a lot of bruises come morning, and he was glad she didn't have long fingernails, as he would have been bloody too.

She finally tired out and settled, crying hard. Stud had never seen this side of her either, and her tears tore at him worse than her hands had. He kissed her temple, murmuring more comforting words, stroking her naked back. He moved down to kiss her ear, tracing the rim with his tongue, feeling her shudder at the contact. Her breathing deepened, and she pressed against him, clinging. He kissed down her neck and shoulder, biting lightly, listening to the soft moan that came from her throat. He tilted his head and held one breast up, teasing her nipple into a tight bud before sucking it deep in his mouth. She gasped and arched her back, offering him better access. He took it, rolling the other in his fingers, switching back and forth between them. He played with her breasts until she was writhing with need. His dick hardened, rising up between her legs, but he ignored it as best he could. This was for her. He got to his knees and pulled one of her thighs over his shoulders, spreading her open to his mouth. He licked at her clit, sucking it gently. She moaned again and pressed into him, asking for more. He gave it. He slid a finger inside her wet opening, hooking it against the secret spot only he knew about in her body. Her muscles clenched at his stroking digit and his dick went rock-hard, feeling her channel grip him. She cried out and came, her juices flowing from her to mingle with the shower stream. Stud licked her sensitive bud of flesh a few more times, then stood, fisting his own cock, and finished himself off against her stomach. The water was starting to grow cold. He washed them off quickly and got them out of the shower, dried off, and into the bed. Clothes could wait.

Stud lay on his back, Eva curled into his side with his arm around her. He stroked her drying hair that was starting to curl and kissed her forehead. Touching her had become such a habit he didn't think about it anymore. A few sounds filtered into the room, other people moving around, a TV turning on, and cars going by. Still, Stud continued to stroke and hold Eva. She was now relaxing and starting to drift off.

"Stay with me," he asked, his voice soft but strong and sure. "Come back to Bryson City and stay with me. I have a condo. Plenty of room for you and your sewing machine. Your lounge pants and other stuff are selling like hot cakes, and I'll help you get the insurance sorted and deal with the legal stuff if they won't pay out. Until that happens, you don't have to make any other decisions right now other than this one."

She shifted, wide awake now. "Fuck my life!" she declared, erupting from the bed. Stud was not expecting it and froze at the sight and feel of her naked body suddenly straddling his. She put her hands on his shoulders as if to hold him down and stared into his eyes.

"I'm over this bullshit. The whole ride to get here, I was hoping for a sign. I wanted to quit the crew and come back with you to Bryson City. I guess I got my sign. A fucking huge one that just had to include a fuckin' bonfire so everyone could see it! I love all my brothers, but Connor is right. The time is way past for us to make our own ways. I can't say what I feel about Da just yet. I'm mad as hell at him, but I know he is who he is and he's not gonna change. Maybe someday I'll get over my house, but right now, I don't want to see or talk to him."

She sat back a bit, her naked core settling on his quickly hardening dick. "Damn! I just wish my Jimmy Choos had survived. I'm gonna miss those shoes!"

Stud could have rejoiced. This was the Eva he knew and loved.

"Are we starting something serious between us? Dare I even ask if this is the R-word you don't like and run from anytime you can? Because right now, I'm not up to dealing with half-ass crap. So you be real sure that's what you want." Her green eyes snapped fire.

Stud's smile became huge. "Yes, I promise you this is serious, Eva," he answered, placing his hands on her hips. "I want you to be in my life and in my bed."

"I will not share," she stated emphatically. "If I move in, it's exclusive. I won't be a scheduled night. No biker bunny Bambis or Nikkis or anyone else. Can you promise me that?"

"Guess threesomes are out," Stud muttered.

"Asshole!" Eva growled, and moved to dismount.

Stud laughed out loud, arched his torso, and flipped her to her back, pushing her legs apart and pressing his throbbing cock between them.

"I'm teasing you, baby. I promise no one else will ever take your place. This is real. This is solid." Stud didn't hesitate.

Eva rolled her hips against his hardness. "Does that make me your old lady?" she asked. "If I have to wear a property patch, that's fine, but I really want to get my own bike. Riding bitch gets old quick."

Stud gave her his half smile as he slid inside her. She took a quick breath at his surprise entry. "Yeah, Cactus, I'll put my patch on you and get you a bike too. You'll need to get on the pill, ASAP. We've been taking a few chances. Not that I'd mind a rug rat or two, but let's get a few years under our belts first."

CHAPTER NINETEEN

THREE MONTHS LATER

S tud settled back into the couch at the Lair, a video game controller in his hands and a beer at his side. Several other brothers were around, him just hanging out. It was a lazy Saturday afternoon in late fall. The weather was cooling off and the leaves were turning the mountains into seas of reds and golds. Eva had gone into town to drop off a load of new sewing projects and to pick up some supplies. Stud knew she would come back with saddlebags full of material. Her lounge pants were flying off the shelves and being shipped around the country just as fast as she could make them. A number of custom quilts had been commissioned and a few local women had asked about dresses as well. The River's

Edge bar was going strong and busy as ever, and the club's other businesses were flourishing. Life was good. Real good, and he hoped nothing would change that.

Eva stomped into the Lair. Clearly, she was pissed as hell. She spotted Stud on the couch and pointed a finger at him.

"You asshole!" she yelled. "This is your fault!"

Stud threw up his hands in defense. "What I'd do?"

One of the guys coughed behind his hand "whipped!"

She stomped over to him and threw something on his lap. "This is what you did, and you did it deliberately!"

She switched to a singsong voice, her eyes fluttering and going all girly-girl for a moment. "Oh, sweetheart, you can't get pregnant so soon after your period. Let's not worry about condoms this time. No probs! Arrgh!"

She switched back to her usual self and crossed her arms in front of her chest. "I can't help it that the pill made me sick and I couldn't take it! You planned this out perfectly, didn't you?"

Stud stared at her fuming face and picked up the white stick sitting near his hardening crotch. Two pink lines met his eyes.

"You're pregnant," he stated calmly, standing.

"Yes, I am! I'm due the same week as that big rally the club goes to every year, and thanks to you, now I can't go! Well, I'm telling you now, *Daddy*, if I can't, then you can't either! Your ass is going to stay right here and hold my hand when I'm in that labor room pushing—"

Stud cut off her tirade by kissing her silent, much to the amusement of the spectators.

"Woooooooh! Stud the man, gonna be a daddy!"

"That's right, buddy! Get her knocked up and keep her that way!"

"Get a room! No wait, you already did! Hahaha!"

Stud said nothing. He pulled a small pouch out of his pocket and opened it. Eva went speechless at the sight of him sliding the huge rock on her left ring finger.

"No place I'd rather be than with you while you give life to our firstborn. Sons are cool, but I want at least one little girl."

"Fuck me sideways!" she breathed, holding up her newly adorned hand.

"Think he already did, darlin'!" came a comment from the couch.

Eva rolled her eyes and tried to recover some of her attitude. Stud loved that about her and smiled his half smile. Eva growled.

"I've got too much stuff going on to plan a big wedding. I hope you don't want it 'cause I'm not doing it! We can get married at the church one afternoon."

Stud chuckled and hugged her close. "You know Betsey, right? Small wedding, my ass! I just have one request, baby."

Eva looked up. "What's that?"

Stud grinned at her. "Instead of carrying a big bunch of flowers, you have to carry a potted plant. A cactus!"

IRISH/GAELIC DEFINITIONS

Fecks: Fools (used to describe someone who has pissed you off)

beag deirfiúr: Little sister

deartháir mór: Big brother

fireann singil: Single man

cailín leisciúil: Lazy girl

Amaideach bodalán: Idiotic asshole

a stóirín: Little darling

mo rún: My love

ACKNOWLEDGMENTS

A big fat thank-you for reading Stud and Eva's story. Stud showed up when I was working on *Mute*, book one and he kept talking to me like he needed his own story. Only a strong woman would be able to handle the Dragon Runner's playboy and thus Eva came to mind.

One issue that sometimes bothers me in book series is when the characters all start looking and sounding the same. This is why I wanted to make a big change with Stud and Eva. In book one, Mute is the bulky, silent, menacing badass type no one wants to be around or mess with, and Kat is the shy, quiet, mousy woman in the corner who would rather not be seen. Somehow they work it out. Stud is the popular, playboy, college-educated man everyone wants a piece of, and Eva is the in-your-face, muscular, blue-collar worker who is not afraid to fight her own battles and will stand up for yours as well.

I think most women can identify with Eva a bit, in that she gets judged by her appearance, her bold attitude, and her occupation. I've dealt with some of that myself in my career as a band instrument repair tech, meaning the field is largely male oriented. My work has been questioned by people more than once because of my gender and not my abilities. This is not a good feeling, but I have to say it's getting better as people are starting to accept women in previously forbidden occupations. There are more women in BIR than ever and they are making a difference to the ones coming into the field. Keep it up!

Speaking of strong women, I have to give a big thank-you to all those ladies who helped bring *Stud* to life. I am very grateful to the beta readers, Brittany Alexander, Barbara Hoover, Franci Neill, Kolleen Fraser, Randie Creamer, and Andrea Robinson for pointing out the details I missed and keeping it real. Liv, you're fantastic! Please be picky! As always, a big thank-you to the Hot Tree Publishing team: Becky, Justine, Donna, and anyone else I might have missed. I couldn't do this without the support of these wonderful women! A big shout out to the sisterhood of bloggers who help promote the work of women authors. Love all of you and I will be eternally grateful for your support! *Ni neart go cur le cheile!* (There is strength in unity).

ABOUT THE AUTHOR

ML Nystrom had stories in her head since she was a child. All sorts of stories of fantasy, romance, mystery, and anything else that captured her interest. A voracious reader, she's spent many hours devouring books; therefore, she found it only fitting she should write a few herself!

ML has spent most of my life as a performing musician and band instrument repair technician, but that doesn't mean she's pigeonholed into one mold. She's been a university professor, belly dancer, craftsperson, soap maker, singer, rock band artist, jewelry maker, lifeguard, swim coach, and whatever else she felt like exploring. As one of her students said to her once, "Life's too short to ignore the opportunities." She has no intention of ever stopping... so welcome to her story world. She hopes you enjoy it!

Facebook: www.facebook.com/authorMLNystrom
Twitter: www.twitter.com/ml_nystrom
Publisher: www.hottreepublishing.com/ml-nystrom

ABOUT THE PUBLISHER

Hot Tree Publishing opened its doors in 2015 with an aspiration to bring quality fiction to the world of readers. With the initial focus on romance and a wide spread of romance subgenres, we envision opening up to alternative genres in the near future.

Firmly seated in the industry as a leading editing provider to independent authors and small publishing houses, Hot Tree Publishing is the sister company to Hot Tree Editing, founded in 2012. Having established in-house editing and promotions, plus having a well-respected market presence, Hot Tree Publishing endeavors to be a leader in bringing quality stories to the world of readers.

Interested in discovering more amazing reads brought to you by Hot Tree Publishing? Head over to the website for information:

WWW.HOTTREEPUBLISHING.COM